THE MURDER BEFORE CHRISTMAS

A WHODUNIT PET COZY MYSTERY SERIES BOOK 4

MEL MCCOY

Copyright © 2019 by Mel McCoy

All rights reserved.

No part of this book may be reproduced in any form or by any electronic or mechanical means, including information storage and retrieval systems, without written permission from the author, except for the use of brief quotations in a book review.

CHAPTER 1

Ten days before Christmas in Cascade Cove, Sarah Shores was in her grandfather's pet shop, Larry's Pawfect Boutique, balancing on the top step of a ladder. A string of Christmas lights hung lazily from her hand as her cousin, Emma, stood at the bottom of the ladder, holding either side.

"We only have about an hour until we open," Emma said.

Sarah clutched the corner of the wall with one hand. "I'm hurrying," she said, trying not to look down. If she did, she'd lose her balance and break her neck, though she turned slightly to take a peek at the clock on the opposite wall. There, she caught a glimpse of Misty, Emma's Persian cat, lying on one of the shelves like an overstuffed ornament while she watched the comedic scene unfold. Sarah turned back and hugged the wall again.

"I don't know why you won't let me do it," Emma said. "You're terrified. I can see it from here."

"I'll never get over my fear of heights if I don't face them." Sarah took a deep breath and tried to focus on the task at hand, rather than the distance between herself and the floor. She peeled herself from the wall slowly and looped the lights around another small hook they'd used the previous years.

"Almost done," she muttered to herself, trying to calm her nerves. She reached further to the right, toward another hook, when a medium-built man in a police uniform walked in. It was Adam Dunkin, an old friend of Sarah's from when she'd come down to Florida from New York every summer as a kid. He was her summer best friend and later, when they became teenagers, her summer crush—though she'd never admitted that to anyone. Now, he was one of Cascade Cove's finest police officers, turned detective as of last week. And she had to admit, seeing him in uniform always gave her butterflies.

She had often thought about the tender embrace and the kiss he gave her on the cheek a few months back, after they'd nabbed the killer of a local artist. Something her cousin Emma had ragged on her about for weeks afterward. But she never talked about it with Adam, and he never brought it up either—perhaps he thought it had been a mistake. So, she'd been acting like it never happened. Though...there were times she'd sworn he was staring at her, and when she'd glanced up, he'd looked away. And he'd made kind gestures often, like picking up coffee for her, or her favorite desserts from Patricia's Tea Room. But those kind gestures could've also been interpreted as just friendly.

Adam looked up at Sarah on the ladder. "Well, well, well. What do we have here?"

"A stubborn lady who is trying to overcome her phobia," Emma said.

"Is that so?" Adam called up to Sarah.

Sarah glanced down at Adam, tightening her grip. "It's not a phobia. It's just a fear," Sarah called down.

"Just like the spiders," Emma said to Adam. "Remember that?"

"Oh, yeah." Adam chuckled. "That summer, she thought if she exposed herself to them more, she'd get over the fear."

Emma laughed. "So she drove to the animal life preserve to get close to a tarantula. The poor guy working there had no idea when he came up behind her and placed it on her shoulder that she would scream like that!"

Adam was holding back so much laughter that his eyes welled up with tears. "I've never seen her move so fast."

"And jump so high. She cleared a table!"

Adam and Emma exploded with laughter.

Sarah glanced at Adam and Emma, who were doubling over. "Ha-ha, you two. Very funny." She bent down to grip the ladder's top platform again, keeping her balance.

"Poor guy," Adam said.

Emma tightened her hold on the ladder to steady it. "Poor spider!"

"I'll have you know that it did help," Sarah said. "I'm not as jumpy with the smaller spiders now." She looped the last light around the final hook. "There! All done!"

Emma and Adam both looked up. Emma, still holding the ladder, said, "The lights are slightly off. They need to sag more on that end." She pointed to the right, where Sarah had just been working.

"First they're sagging too much, now they're not sagging enough." Sarah reached over to the last rung and fixed it. "Is that better?"

"Much better."

Sarah let out a sigh of relief and slowly made her way down the ladder.

Adam greeted her at the bottom. "You never seem that scared on the Ferris wheel."

"That's different," Sarah said, still shaking slightly.

"Of course, it is," Emma said, trying to find the other end of the lights to plug it into the wall socket. "I just don't see how."

"On the Ferris wheel, I'm sitting and locked in," Sarah said. "And I'm not looking straight down. Not to mention, how could I ever deprive myself of the beautiful ocean view and the horizon from up there? It's simply breathtaking." The image of the sun setting behind the water flashed through Sarah's mind, and she wished she could be on the Ferris wheel now—too bad it was closed for the off-season.

Emma plugged in the strand of white, twinkling lights. The three of them stood back, admiring them.

"They're beautiful," Sarah said.

"So, how does it feel putting up Christmas decorations in seventy-degree weather?" Adam asked.

This was the first Christmas Sarah would be spending in Florida since she'd left her apartment in New York a few months ago, leaving her old life behind. She'd been a teacher, helping kids in an inner-city school, but because of the politics within the school system and faculty, her hands had been tied tighter and tighter and her stress levels had gone through the roof.

She'd gone days without sleep, trying to beat the system. That was before she'd decided to make a life change. After a beautiful and relaxing summer with her family and friends, not to mention nabbing three killers in the past six months and helping improve her grandfather's pet boutique, she felt like she was doing more good in Cascade Cove than in the city and had decided to move in with her grandparents and cousin above Larry's Pawfect Boutique.

"To be honest," Sarah said, "it's kind of weird. I feel like I'm living in an alternate universe."

Adam grinned. "You'll get used to it. We still do all the Christmasy things like decorating and putting up lights. You might come across several pink flamingos with Santa hats, and instead of snow angels, we make sand angels. But other than that, it's the same."

Sarah shook her head. "As much as I'd love to see a flamingo in a Santa hat, I don't think sand angels could take the place of white, glistening snow angels."

"I promise you, you will come across a flamingo in a Santa hat this Christmas. It's so rare not to that it's actually bad luck if you don't."

"Well then, I hope to see one soon. We don't need any bad luck here."

Adam chuckled. "No. No, we don't. We also have the annual Surfing Santas the Saturday before Christmas.

Now that, you cannot miss out on. I would think that's bad luck in itself," he said, waggling his eyebrows.

Sarah laughed, but inside, it really didn't feel like Christmas. She never thought she'd miss the frigid temperatures of New York City, but she missed the boots and sweaters, thick socks and hot beverages. She missed nuzzling her chin into a warm, chunky scarf. Though the warmer weather hadn't stopped her from knitting dog sweaters every night to sell in the shop and her grandfather's online store, she had no use for knitting sweaters for herself or friends.

"So, Adam," Sarah said. "What brings you here bright and early this morning?"

"I wanted to stop by and give you the news."

"What news?"

"You'll never guess who's here in town."

"Rufus," Emma said, grabbing a box of ornaments. She made her way over to the corner of the shop, to the Christmas tree that stood bare. "He comes every year around this time with his family." Emma put a finger to her chin. "Though, isn't this supposed to be his last show? I think he's retiring this year."

"Who's Rufus?" Sarah asked.

"He's a magician. Don't tell me you've never heard of him. You know, the magnificent Rufus?"

Sarah stared at him blankly.

Adam dropped his shoulders in defeat. "He'd make people in the audience come up on stage, and he'd make them disappear. It was huge."

"Oh, that guy. Yeah, that was way back when I was, like, ten years old."

"Yeah," Emma said. "Rufus comes back to town every year, and Grandpa goes through his magician phase every time."

"That's right," Adam said with a chuckle. "You're never here this time of year to see Grandpa Larry's magic tricks."

"I love magic," Sarah said. "Why hasn't he ever showed me one of his tricks?"

Emma raised an eyebrow. "Like we said, it's a phase. Just like the annual sandcastle competition, the trumpet, the harmonica—"

Adam snapped his finger and pointed to Emma. "Or the hula hoop competition."

Emma rolled her eyes. "Oh, yeah. Almost forgot about that one. He almost won, too."

"Well, I like a good magic trick," Sarah said.

"Of course, but don't expect much. He's not very good."

Sarah regarded Adam. "So, how does it feel to be one of Cascade Cove's detectives?"

Adam shook his head. "I still have the same duties I

did before, only now I have a nice title to carry with me while performing those jobs."

Sarah laughed.

"Anyway," Adam started, "would you ladies like to run over to Patricia's Tea Room and grab some key lime bars?"

Emma glanced at the wall clock. "We'll be opening in about a half hour. I want to get some more of the decorations up. You two go."

"Are you sure?" Sarah asked.

Emma waved her hand at them as if to shoo them out. "Yeah, go. Someone has to man the store and keep Misty company until Grandpa and the pups get back."

"Where is Larry?" Adam asked.

"He's taking the dogs for a walk," Sarah said. "Says he needs to start exercising more, and the dogs are a good excuse to get him out." She shifted her gaze to her cousin. "Do you want us to pick you up anything?"

Emma opened one of the cardboard boxes that contained what appeared to be garland. "Sure, key lime bars sound pretty good, actually."

"You got it."

Adam held the door open for Sarah, and they made their way down the street to Patricia's Tea Room. Patricia was a long-time friend of her grandmother's, since they'd opened shop about thirty-five years ago. On top of that, Patricia also had a granddaughter named Nancy who was Sarah's age and helped at the Tea Room. She'd also begun taking care of Patricia herself, since the day she had a small heart attack that landed her in the hospital earlier that year. Now, Nancy was taking care of all the day-to-day work at the Tea Room, doing all the front end work while Patricia rested in the back. It had been a while since they'd seen Patricia.

When they reached the Tea Room, Sarah's eyebrows rose. Patricia's was still bustling, even during the off-season, but of course, these people were all regulars—folks who lived in the area. It was like family there.

They walked in, and the smell of spice and sugary treats filled Sarah's nose. The sweet aroma made her feel warm inside, and she smiled. Adam ushered Sarah to the counter. A woman in her mid-thirties sashayed between the tables to make her way to them, her ponytail swaying to and fro as she walked.

"Hey, Nancy," Adam said, placing his hands on the countertop. "How's Patricia?"

Nancy smiled. "She's doing very well. Her heart is stronger than ever, and she's been up and about lately—more than I'd like, sometimes."

Just then, Patricia came out from the back. When she saw them, her eyes lit up. "Sarah and Adam!" she said as she darted around the counter, briskly walking up toward Sarah with outstretched arms. "Oh, Sarah!" The petite elderly woman gave her a tight hug, her rosy perfume's pleasant scent melding with the smell of the baked goods.

After she released Sarah, Patricia turned to Adam. "Get your big ol' handsome self over here. You're never too big to get a hug from me." She squeezed him, and when their hug ended, Patricia touched Adam's bicep. "My, my, Adam. Have you been working out?"

"Mrs. Greensmith," Adam said, "if I didn't know any better, I'd think you were flirting with me."

Patricia laughed. "Can't blame an old woman for doing so." She looked him up and down and said, "Look at you." Then she nudged Sarah, leaning into her and shielding her mouth with her hand so that Adam couldn't see her lips. "You might want to nail this one down before he gets away."

Sarah chuckled.

Patricia stepped back, looking Adam over once more. "What a stud!"

It was amazing how energetic Patricia was. Last time Sarah had seen her, she'd struggled to get up on her feet. Now, she was walking and waving her arms around like she was half her age.

"Okay, Nana," Nancy said. "That's enough. Why don't you go sit, and I'll bring you some tea."

"I don't need to sit. I just got up from sitting. Let me take care of Sarah and Adam, and *you* sit. I need to get back to work anyway, so you can go find yourself a nice young man and settle down. I hear Adam here is available."

Nancy punched her fists into her hips. "Nana!"

"All right," Adam said. "Mrs. Greensmith—"

"Adam!" Patricia's eyebrows furrowed. "When did you start using formalities with me?"

Adam held up his hands by his chest in defense. "Sorry, Patricia."

Patricia's face relaxed. "That's better."

Adam tried again. "Listen, Patricia's right. I think she should take our order." He gave Nancy a wink.

Nancy dropped her hands by her sides. "Okay," she said with a smirk. Then she turned to her nana. "But take it easy, especially with the flirting."

"Someone's got to do it, since neither one of you two ladies are," Patricia mumbled.

Nancy chuckled and shook her head before walking away to take care of another table.

Patricia went behind the counter, pulling her signature blue apron on, with the Patricia's Tea Room teacup and saucer logo on it. "So, what would you two like?"

"Two key lime bars and two to go," Sarah said.

"Two to go?" Adam asked.

Sarah looked at Adam. "Yes, one for Emma and one for Grandpa when he gets back from his walk."

"What about tea?" Patricia asked.

"Oh, I don't know what I want." Sarah glanced at the menu behind Patricia, scanning the list of teas.

"I'll just get you the tea of the day."

"That sounds perfect."

"Great! Take a seat at one of the tables, and I'll get it for you."

"Thanks, Patricia."

Sarah and Adam found an empty table in the back corner, since all the window seats were taken. She sat down with her back facing the wall so she could see the entire room and the windows and adjusted herself so that she was comfortable. A man wearing a flat cap and a tweed suit with a bright-red handkerchief in the front pocket of his jacket ambled his way to the counter. Sarah leaned forward to see who was at the counter to take his order and was relieved to see it was Nancy and not Patricia. Even though Patricia seemed much better —more than better—she still worried about her and didn't want her to overdo it. She leaned back into her chair.

"Are you all right?" Adam asked.

"Yeah, just wanted to make sure that Patricia was taking it easy."

Adam nodded. "I worry about her too."

"There's no need to worry about me," Patricia said, placing their desserts in front of them on the table.

Sarah jumped at her voice—the woman seemed to have appeared out of nowhere. "Wow, Patricia, that was fast," she said, putting a hand to her chest to calm her heart, which was now thumping quickly.

"Fast? All I had to do was grab two bars and put them each on a plate and pour some tea. It's not that complicated, nor time consuming, sweetie," Patricia said with a chuckle. "I still have to wrap up the other bars to go." Patricia paused a moment, looking at both of them. "It's so nice to see you two again. Actually, it's nice to be out here and with everyone again. I really did miss you."

"Thanks, Patricia. We really missed you, too. And we're so glad you're feeling better."

"I really have Nancy to thank for that. She is a true sweetheart."

"That, she is," Adam said.

When Patricia disappeared, Sarah took a sip of her tea. The man in the jacket was now walking briskly toward the door, his head down as if trying to conceal his face. Something was off about the man, like he was hiding something. Sarah followed him with her eyes as he made his way out the door and out of sight.

CHAPTER 2

When Adam and Sarah walked through the door of the Pawfect Boutique, Emma was sitting at the desk, typing away at the computer. Misty was nestled on Emma's left shoulder, leaning against the back of the chair, purring in cozy bliss.

Emma looked up from the screen and smiled. "Hey! Back already?" Glancing at the clock hanging above their heads, her smile quickly turned to surprise. "Oh boy, look at the time! We open in five minutes, and I have all these boxes to put away."

Sarah and Adam walked up to the counter, and Adam set the bag of key lime bars next to her computer. Sarah rushed over to one of the empty decoration boxes. "Let me help you," she said, picking it up.

"I'll help, too," Adam said.

"Thank you." Emma was already scurrying around, collecting boxes. In the midst of the rush, the bells jingled over the door. Sarah thought it was a customer, but when she heard the fumbling of a yellow lab and a corgi, she knew it was Grandpa.

"Top of the morning!" Grandpa Larry said as he walked in. Then he paused, still holding the leashes to two spunky, ecstatic canines. He scanned the boutique, taking off his straw hat. "What happened in here? Looks like Christmas just threw up all over the shop!" He chuckled.

"We thought we could get the decorations up before we opened today," Emma explained. "But, unfortunately, that wasn't the case."

Larry glanced at the tree. "I see the tree is still naked."

Emma jutted out her hip and placed her hand on it, while giving her grandfather an unamused look.

"Uh, anyway," Larry continued, "never mind about that. You'll never guess who's in town."

"Rufus," Sarah and Emma said in unison.

"How'd you all know?"

Emma grabbed another box and carried it behind the counter. "Grandpa, he comes every year around this time."

"Oh, right," Larry said, unhooking the two anxious

pups. As soon as the fumbling yellow lab was released, he darted toward Adam, wiggling and licking his hand.

"Rugby," Sarah said in a warning tone. At the sound of his name, the yellow lab sat down and looked back at her, with his body still facing Adam. "Mind your manners."

Rugby turned back to Adam and panted. Adam bent over and rubbed behind the dog's ears playfully. "Who's a good dog?" Adam asked Rugby, who gave an enthusiastic whine in response.

"Now you're going to get him all wound up," Sarah said, folding her arms at her chest.

"Nah, he's a good boy," Adam said, looking up at Sarah. But before he could say anything else, Rugby jumped up and placed both front paws on Adam's chest, knocking him off balance. Adam fell back, the blond furry body of Rugby smothering him.

Sarah rushed over. "Adam! Are you all right?" Rugby was on top of him, licking his face as Adam tried to shield himself with both arms. Sarah took a step back, and with her deepest tone, called Rugby's name and said, "Off!" Rugby turned his head toward her before climbing off Adam.

"Come!" she demanded. Rugby headed toward her, his tail wagging gleefully. When he was at Sarah's feet, he sat without her command.

Adam was now sitting on the ground and laughing as he wiped the yellow lab's kisses off of his face. "Well, I guess he's really happy to see me."

Sarah shook her head and sighed. "I'm sorry, Adam."

Adam rose to his feet. "Don't be. He just took me off guard. He's still a good boy."

"Try taking him for a walk," Larry said.

"I thought he was walking better for you," Sarah said.

Larry shrugged. "He is, but I'd still like to see Adam take him for a walk."

"That's why I like cats," Emma said as she put the last box away.

Sarah laughed. The corgi, Winston, tottered over to them, his heart-shaped butt waddling to and fro, before sitting beside Sarah's feet. Sarah gave him a pat on the head. "Winston here is good."

The corgi was a rescue that found Sarah the first week she was in Cascade Cove for the summer. She had seen him on the boardwalk carrying an antique locket. A storm was approaching that night, and Sarah couldn't locate his owner, so she had decided to bring him into the shop to avoid the downpour. After that, the corgi followed her everywhere she went. Later, she adopted him after learning he had run away from the Cozy Beachside Rescue Center in Filbertsville, the next town over, where he had been waiting for someone to adopt him into a forever home. Sarah felt more than lucky that she was the one to provide a forever home for him in Cascade Cove.

Adam looked at his phone. "Well, I better get down to the station. Thanks for another eventful morning." Then he pointed at Rugby. "And you, stay out of trouble."

Rugby gave two short barks, as if he understood Adam, and they all laughed.

"I'll catch you later," Adam said to Sarah with a wink before walking out the door.

Sarah's face flushed, and she tried to hide it by turning away from her cousin and Grandpa, pretending to adjust the stuffed dog toys on a rack behind her. "We should open the store now. We're late."

"That's a good idea," Larry said, and he darted to the door that led to the upstairs apartment.

"Where are you going?" Sarah asked.

"I want to find my magic books. I need to brush up on my performance."

Emma shook her head.

"Maybe I can get tickets to Rufus's show this time, before they sell out!" Larry said, before disappearing out the door.

"Maybe we should start decorating the tree," Emma said. She was staring at the medium-sized artificial Christmas tree that Larry had put together—he had it stored away in a large, rectangular box eleven months out of the year, but now, after hours of finagling to get the "branches" just so, the tree looked somewhat realistic.

"Yeah," Sarah said, stepping toward the tree. "It's not like we're bustling with customers." It was amazing how quiet the town was without the vacationers. At this rate, the season was going to be a long and dull one.

Emma stood, retrieving a box of ornaments, and carried it to Sarah. "Here, you can start with these."

Sarah opened the box, revealing different types of dog and cat ornaments dressed up in holiday-themed attire. She reached in and picked up a white poodle in a red and green sweater, holding a candy cane in its mouth. "These are adorable," she said, hanging it on the tree.

Emma carried another box over and placed it in front of the tree, opening it. "Grandpa and I picked them out. You can help next time."

Sarah pulled out another ornament. This time it was a British shorthair blue cat with a wreath—she hung it six inches away from the poodle. "Where'd you get these?" she asked as she held up a miniature Dalmatian wearing an elf costume.

"We have a catalog filled with stuff like this. Believe it or not, we actually sell many of these ornaments—these are kind of our 'display models.' People love them, and we sell a ton every year. Last year, we ran out and had to start selling them right off the tree."

"Really? But it seems like it has really slowed down since Halloween."

"Don't worry," Emma said, opening another box of ornaments. "It will pick back up by next week. Even Mrs. Jacobs comes in every year and buys a bunch of these to give away as gifts for Christmas."

"Wow. Does Mrs. Jacobs even have a pet?"

"Nope. But her entire family does," Emma said with a chuckle. "And on top of that, this year, we have a section on the website devoted to holiday items. I'm getting a few more shipments of these ornaments later this week, so hopefully we don't run out until then. Soon, you'll see how much we need you during the off-season, too."

"Just as long as I'm not a burden."

"A burden? No way. Far from it."

Hopefully, her cousin wasn't just saying that to make Sarah feel better, but it still helped. Sarah reached into the box, and this time, she pulled out another ornament to place on the tree.

It only took them about an hour to decorate the entire tree and stow the boxes away. Then Emma, struggling a bit, brought out another box. This one was much bigger than the boxes she'd had out for the ornaments.

"What's that?" Sarah asked.

"This is for the front window."

Sarah tilted her head to one side. "But we already did the garland and lights around the windows."

Emma pulled the big flaps of the box open. "This isn't garland. This is Grandpa's pride and joy." She slowly undressed a forty-eight-inch sculpture of a puppy with a big red bow around its neck. It was made of wire and glittery thread with white LED lights weaved into it.

Sarah stared, wide-eyed. "Wow! That is absolutely beautiful."

"Yeah, I got it for him for Christmas a few years ago. I set it up in the front window and had it all lit and ready to go for when he came down to see it. He loves this thing. Here," Emma said, picking up the front end of the dog. "Help me. You get the back end." She pointed toward the dog's rear.

"Thanks," Sarah said with a smirk. She helped Emma place it on the wide sill of the front window of the shop. "It's really light."

"Yeah, it's made of just thin wire and thread." Emma

grabbed the cord and plugged it into a receptacle in the wall. The dog lit up brightly.

"It's even more beautiful when it's all lit up," Sarah said. "The white lights match the lights of the tree, and the big red bow and the silver bells around its neck are a really nice touch."

"It even plays Christmas tunes. Watch this." Emma tilted the sculpture to show a button under the dog's paw. "The speaker is inside the dog, but because it's made of thin strands of wire woven loosely together, the music comes out unmuffled." She flipped the switch and "We Wish You a Merry Christmas" began to play.

"That is too cute."

"Yeah," Emma said. "Now help me with this box. I want to get it in the back before our afternoon rush starts."

Sarah scurried over to her cousin and grabbed the opposite end of the box. Together, they dragged it into the back room.

"There," Emma said, clapping her hands together to remove any dust. "That should do it."

Emma closed the door to the back room and put the key in the knob to lock it, when the bells above the door jingled. A tall man was towering in the doorway, blocking the sun rays and casting a long, dark shadow into the store. He was wearing a black, three-piece suit and an abundance of chunky gold jewelry around his thick neck and fingers. He took his top hat off, revealing a head of thinning red hair. His groomed beard was graying, showing signs of aging, and he wore a scowl as he eyed up Emma and Sarah.

Emma's mouth dropped. "It's Rufus," she whispered to Sarah. "Rufus the Magnificent."

CHAPTER 3

Rufus the Magnificent stood there a moment at the doorway, scanning the room, red leash in hand. Sarah followed the leash to see a Jack Russell at the end of it. The dog noticed Sarah and Emma and let out a bark.

"Quiet, Houdini," Rufus said in a baritone voice. The little Jack Russell terrier whined as it tore its gaze from them. Rufus wandered to the other side of the store, dragging the dog with him.

"He walks better if you don't drag him," said a man who was coming in right behind Rufus. He resembled the tall man with his thinning red hair, but he was skinnier, clean shaven, and wasn't going bald. At least, not yet.

"I'm not dragging him." Rufus tried to walk the dog

again, but Houdini seemed more interested in saying hello to Sarah and Emma. "Here," Rufus said, shoving the leash toward the other man. "If you think he'll walk better for you, then take the mutt."

The man sighed, grasping the leash. "He's not a mutt. He's a purebred." Then he glanced down at the dog. "C'mon, Houdini. Let's look at all the toys."

Rufus huffed, shoving his hands into his pockets and sauntering around aimlessly.

"That's definitely Rufus," Emma said, nodding her head. "I've seen his picture every year on posters. Though, I've never seen him in person before."

The man was slightly intimidating.

Then two women entered, who also resembled each other. One had curly blonde hair tied up in a high bun, and the other had straight blonde hair, hanging just above her shoulders, and bangs.

The woman with bangs walked over to them, checking out the dog toys by the counter.

"Is that Rufus the Magnificent?" Sarah asked the woman.

The woman smiled. "What gave it away? The top hat?" She let out a chuckle, then put out her hand. "I'm Judy Hattingsford. I'm Rufus's wife."

Sarah shook the lady's hand. "Very nice to meet you. I'm Sarah, and this is my cousin, Emma."

Emma and Judy shook hands.

Judy pointed at the shorter man who was next to Rufus, looking at the Christmas tree. "That's Buster—"

Emma's eyes grew wide. "Isn't he the Bold and Brilliant Buster?"

Judy laughed. "Yeah, that's him. Now known as the Bombastic Buster, ever since his teleportation trick failed twenty years ago."

"Who's the lady with him? Is that his wife?"

"Oh, gosh, no. That's my twin sister, Faith Hartlob. She's single. She just likes to keep me company while Rufus is performing. She travels with us. We've always been real close."

"Are you looking for anything in particular?" Emma asked.

"No, we're just making our rounds. Faith and I saw that this was a pet boutique and figured Houdini might like it."

"You mean, the dog," Sarah said, more as a statement of clarification than an actual question. The white Jack Russell scurried across the floor next to Buster, sniffing every nook and cranny he could find. He had the most endearing markings—brown around one eye, yet his other eye remained white. Both of his small, folded ears were also brown, with one big brown spot on his back.

"Yeah, he's the family pet," Judy said. "We saw the

Christmas dog in the window. Kind of resembles our Houdini."

"Yeah," Emma said, nodding in agreement. "He kind of does."

"After this," Judy continued, "we'll probably try out one of the restaurants around here. Houdini loves a good burger. Any suggestions?"

"We love the Banana Hammock. It's just down the boardwalk a little ways from here." Emma pointed to the direction of their favorite restaurant, one they'd frequented probably too many times with their grandfather.

"Thanks for the recommendation. We'll definitely have to try that."

"So, I hear Rufus has his big last show coming up next week," Emma said to Judy.

"Friday," Judy said. "It's about time he retires. Been waiting for this for years."

"Is he nervous?"

"No, he's performed shows so many times, he could do them in his sleep. He's more worried about his assistant. Bebe Binkerton isn't with him anymore, so he's been scrambling to find a new leading lady."

"Oh, boy," Sarah said. "And so close to the show. I hope it all works out for him."

"I'm sure it will," Judy said. "It always does."

"How long are you planning on staying in Cascade Cove?" Emma asked.

"Well, after the show, we are going to do some sight-seeing. We'll probably walk along the beach. We own the beach house down past the pier."

"I heard," Emma said. "The blue house right by the Beachside Beacon."

Judy aimed a thin index finger at Emma. "Yeah, that's the one. Rufus loves the Beacon. He likes to walk around that area often."

"Do be careful. There are a lot of big rocks by the Beacon. Sometimes the water gets treacherous and those rocks get rather slippery."

The doorbell jingled again, and a small boy rushed in with his mother trailing behind. He scanned the boutique until he zeroed in on Rufus. "There he is, Mom," the boy said over his shoulder. "I knew I saw him go in here!"

"Well, why don't you ask him, then?" the mother said.

The boy nodded, then cautiously approached the famed magician. "Um, excuse me, sir…"

Rufus whipped around, peering down at the boy. His scowl remained. "What do you want?"

"I, uh…I was…"

"Out with it. You're wasting my time."

"Could you…uh, do a magic trick?"

The corners of Sarah's mouth ticked upward. They were all going to be in for a treat. A famous magician was going to wow everyone in the shop with a fun little trick, perhaps a standard slight-of-hand that he whipped up each time he was asked this particular question.

"Magic trick?" Rufus asked, his scowl intensifying. "If you want a magic trick, you should buy a ticket to my upcoming show, like everyone else. No freebies!"

The boy's lower lip quivered, and he rushed back over to his mother. "What's the matter with you?" the mother called over to Rufus. "You didn't have to treat him like that—he's just a boy!"

Rufus set his steely gaze on the woman. "What do you do for a living, ma'am?"

The woman stammered a moment out of pure frustration and bewilderment at the question before she responded. "I write children's books."

"Well, then… if you don't mind, why don't you write me a two-thousand-word short story about a magician who wants to be left alone. Submit it to me after I'm finished browsing."

The woman's face flushed bright red.

Rufus continued, "I suppose you think my request is out of line?"

"Uh, yes, but…" the woman said, certainly understanding the magician's point.

"Well, then, now you know how I feel. Tickets are twenty-five dollars each. You can purchase them on my website. Now, if you'll excuse me, I'll be enjoying my time off the clock, just as you are enjoying your time not writing what I'm assuming are dreadful stories."

The woman's scowl matched the magician's for a moment, and she took her child's hand. "Come on, Billy. We won't be supporting such an absurdly horrible man." She gave the magician one final glare before storming out of the boutique, dragging her son along with her.

"Good!" Rufus said after her.

"Rufus," Judy said, her mouth agape. "Was that necessary?"

The magician turned to his wife, who shook her head. "Ta da," he said, scowl now replaced by a mischievous grin. "I made that miserable woman disappear."

Sarah exchanged a glance with her cousin, trying to suppress her shock.

"I think it's time to go," Judy said, regarding Sarah and Emma. "I'm awfully sorry. Rufus has just been feeling...uh...under the weather lately."

Rufus harrumphed. "I'll say when it's time to go."

Judy hung her hands at her side in defeat.

Rufus looked around, then his eyes stopped on his wife's. "I'd like to go now. Not because you said so, but because I feel like it." He looked at the other two people that had walked in with him and said, "Let's go."

Judy mouthed "sorry" once more before trailing behind them and the Jack Russell out the door.

Sarah and Emma looked at one another again, baffled by what had just happened.

"So, that's Rufus the Magnificent," Sarah said. She walked over to the door and looked out the glass to catch a final glimpse of the man and his family strolling down the boardwalk and out of sight. She turned to her cousin, who was still standing behind the counter. "What a treat he is."

"Good thing Grandpa wasn't here to witness that," Emma said, shaking her head. "I think it would have depressed him. He loves that guy. Admires him, in fact."

Sarah peered out the window again, and her brows wrinkled in surprise—across the street stood the man she'd just seen at Patricia's Tea Room, with the flat hat and tweed suit. The man wasn't dressed like a resident of Cascade Cove. And the red handkerchief tucked in his front pocket didn't match his attire.

She squinted to get a better look. He was talking to another man, who had an awkward smile. He wore a hat, too—not a flat cap, but a regular cap and sunglasses. She couldn't tell if they were friendly or not, but it seemed like they might've known each other.

"Sarah, what are you looking at?" Emma asked.

The man with the sunglasses pointed at something behind the flat cap guy, and he turned to look back. Sarah couldn't help but notice the big gold ring on the man's finger as he pointed. When the flat cap guy turned back around, the other man shrugged. They continued talking to one another.

"This guy," Sarah said, gesturing toward the window. "He doesn't look like he's from around here."

Emma walked over and looked out the window. After a moment she turned to Sarah. "I don't see anyone."

Sarah took another peek. She looked to the left and then the right. The two men had disappeared. Then she crinkled her forehead and let out a quick breath through her nostrils. "Hmm, that's strange."

CHAPTER 4

The next morning, Sarah was in the kitchen with her cousin, waiting for the coffee maker to brew a fresh pot of cheap grocery-store coffee. It was a routine that usually involved Grandpa, but he was fast asleep during the gloomy morning. Sarah couldn't blame him, but someone had to get up and tend to the store. As the coffee maker was puffing and gurgling, Sarah and Emma stood there, mugs in hand, ready to fight for the first cup.

Sarah had mentioned getting a single-serve coffee maker, but both Grandma and Emma had argued that the K-cups were far too expensive. When Sarah did her own price check, she realized they were right. And so, since then, they had opted to continue living in the dark ages with an old thirty-dollar coffee maker that took its time to create the watered-down beverage.

Sarah gave a big, well-deserved yawn. It was an overcast morning, and she couldn't quite wake herself up fully on these kinds of days. Even the dogs were lounging in their beds, lazy yet comfy and warm. "So much for the Sunshine State."

Emma, still watching the pot, said, "Well, even Florida has its bad days." Misty jumped up on the stool next to the counter at which they were standing. She purred loudly, bumping her head into Emma's arm. "All right, all right," Emma said, petting her. "I get it. You need attention."

As Emma rubbed Misty's head and scratched behind her ears, the coffee maker coughed the last few drops it had left into the pot. Despite her divided attention, Emma was quicker; she grabbed the handle and poured herself a cup.

Sarah blamed her slower reflexes on the gloomy day. After Emma was done, Sarah then poured herself some coffee, too, adding milk and sugar. "So, what's on the agenda for today?"

"Grandpa or no Grandpa, I want to get started on the end-of-year inventory count."

"Good idea," Sarah said, stirring her coffee. "Can't

wait to get started." She clinked her small spoon on the edge of the ceramic mug to rid the excess coffee from it and set the spoon down. Bringing the cup to her lips, she took a sip.

Emma chuckled mischievously. "I admire your enthusiasm, but I don't think you understand how bad end-of-year inventory really is. But by the time we're done, I'm sure you'll truly appreciate how awful and monotonous it is."

Sarah had done the inventory count with Emma before. Sure, it wasn't a glamorous job, and it wasn't much fun, but that was why it was called a job. How bad could it really be?

A few minutes later, Sarah was adding food to Winston's and Rugby's dishes as they came skirting around the corner, ready to quickly devour their morning breakfast of dry kibble. Per usual, Rugby scarfed up his entire breakfast in one fell swoop and then clumsily gallivanted over to Sarah to get some morning belly rubs.

When Sarah was done giving Rugby the attention he needed, they headed down to the boutique to start the dreaded inventory job, Rugby and Winston trailing behind them. When they walked in, Sarah flipped the switch that turned on all the lights in the boutique, including the newly hung Christmas lights, but only half of the beautiful, twinkling white lights on the wall above the entrance and the counter were working.

They both stopped in their tracks.

Emma dropped her shoulders. "Boo," she said. "Looks like we're going to have to check each light to see which one is the dud that's causing the problem."

Sarah's heart immediately lodged itself into her throat. Just the mere thought of standing at the top of the ladder again sent her circulatory system into a malfunctioning disaster on overload.

Emma must've been feeling Sarah's blood pressure rising. "Don't worry," she said. "I'll get up on the ladder and check them." Emma walked to the door behind the counter, and moments later, was hauling out the ladder, propping it up against the wall to where the first set of lights were dark. "I told Grandpa that these lights were getting old and that we should get new ones, but no," she said to no one in particular. "He never listens to me." Then she turned to Sarah. "Could you hold the ladder for me?"

"Of course." Sarah walked over and gripped each leg of the ladder.

Emma climbed up, still mumbling to herself. She started finagling with each individual bulb and retrieved an extra bulb from her pocket, popping each bulb out and trying the new one in its place, but the lights were still dead. After about twenty minutes of messing with the lights, Emma popped in the new bulb in place of one of the old lights, and the room lit up.

Emma pulled herself back, still holding on to the ladder.

Sarah grinned. "You did it!"

Emma looked down at her cousin on the floor and flashed a smile. "Fixed!" she said, climbing down.

Rugby, who had been lying on the floor patiently, began to whine.

"Mind your manners," Sarah said, wagging a finger at him.

"Grandpa usually has them out for a walk by this time," Emma said, looking at the clock. "We don't open for another hour. Maybe we should just take them and allow Grandpa to sleep."

Sarah nodded. "Good idea." She walked over to where their leashes were nestled in a drawer behind the counter. As soon as Winston and Rugby heard the jingling of their leads, they both perked up, and Rugby galloped in circles. Winston sat like a handsome young pup, with his big ears facing forward. Once Sarah had them both securely clipped to their leads, she handed

Emma Winston's leash, and Sarah took Rugby's. Rugby was a bit more rambunctious than his brother corgi.

They made their way onto the boardwalk, Emma locking the door behind them, and continued off to the left toward Jacobs' Pier, where Sarah had solved her first murder. The seagulls were changing course, and the wind was intensifying as the clouds swirled in the sky up ahead.

"Looks like we're about to get a storm," Sarah said.

Emma looked up, "Nah, this is normal for this time of year. It's the end of hurricane season, so you don't have to worry. Just a little rain later, I presume."

Sarah nodded.

"I just hope the weather is good for the annual Surfing Santa competition," Emma muttered.

"Oh yeah," Sarah said. She'd been looking forward to the event since she heard about it months ago from Teek. It was a tradition in Cascade Cove that other beaches in Florida and other islands had ripped off from them, making it popular nationwide. People from all over came to see the surfing Santas, and Sarah couldn't wait to experience such a fun event herself for the first time.

They went past the pier and continued on for fifteen minutes before they decided to turn around, since they were getting close to the end of the boardwalk.

"When does the competition start?" Sarah asked.

"Early morning," Emma said. "People start crowding the beach at 6:30 a.m."

"That early?"

"Yeah, and it lasts almost all day! I'm sure those surfing Santas get tired."

"I bet," Sarah said. "Though, I wonder—"

She was interrupted by a blood-curdling scream off to their left, toward the beach.

Rugby barked in the direction of the commotion, and Winston whined, both dogs focused on the blue house by the Beachside Beacon.

They heard it again. Another scream.

Sarah and Emma exchanged glances before taking off in a sprint toward the horrendous screams, both dogs in tow. Within seconds, Sarah saw a blonde woman dressed in a white gown that rippled aggressively in the stormy wind. She dropped to her knees as Sarah approached her. Sarah lightly touched the woman's shoulder, and when she turned her head, Sarah instantly recognized her.

"Judy?" Sarah asked. The magician's wife, who'd come into the shop just the day before, seemed to be in total shock. "What's wrong?"

Judy pointed at something laying in a dark heap atop one of the boulders on the terrain.

Rugby went wild, barking incessantly as he pulled on his lead. Sarah planted both feet on the ground in an attempt to pull him back, but his force was incontrollable. They inched closer, and Sarah and Emma craned their necks to see what the woman was pointing at.

Sarah's voice came out in a mere whisper. "Is that Rufus the Magnificent?"

CHAPTER 5

Adam and his partner, Officer Finley, arrived at the scene in record time. After evaluating the body, Sarah told Adam what had happened while Officer Finley took pictures of the scene. Buster and Faith had come running out of the blue beachside house soon after Sarah and Emma had arrived. Now, they were all standing around in a small circle. Sarah struggled to keep Rugby from pulling on his leash, but eventually got him to sit and stay. Winston, on the other hand, sat next to Emma the entire time while Adam asked Rufus's family a few more questions.

"Now, let's start from the top, Mrs. Hattingsford," Adam said. "When's the last time you saw your husband?"

Buster stood next to Faith, who was consoling her

sister. She had her arm wrapped around her as Judy dabbed her eyes with a tissue. "Well, my husband went for a walk last night and I went to bed," Judy said. "When I woke up, I noticed his side of the bed was untouched. I thought maybe he had gotten up early and made his side. Though that would be out of character for him, since he never makes the bed. So, I went downstairs expecting to see him in the kitchen, but he wasn't there. I searched around and figured maybe he went out by the Beacon." Judy sniffed back some tears.

"Take your time, Mrs. Hattingsford."

Judy nodded, tucking her blonde hair behind her ears. Her thin bangs were a bit too long, falling into her eyes. She folded her arms in front of her and continued, "It's his favorite spot." She paused. "Or *was*," she corrected herself. "I looked around, but I didn't see him. I was about to turn back to the house when I saw a black heap on the ground by the rocky terrain. When I stepped closer, I realized it was a body, lying on the rocks. I saw the blood on the back of his head, and I turned him over to see his face." Judy's bottom lip trembled, her eyes welling up. "That's when I realized that it was my husband, and I screamed."

"Okay, Mrs. Hattingsford," Adam said, quickly scratching some more notes into his notepad.

"Judy. You can call me Judy."

"Okay, Judy." Adam flashed a soft smile, but his eyes remained serious.

Just then, another police cruiser pulled up, and Sheriff Wheeler stepped out. He was a hefty fellow with thinning hair and a big, shiny badge clipped to the front of his uniform. At first, Sarah didn't recognize the sheriff. He used to have a graying beard, but it was now gone —shaved off. The sheriff let out a huff as he cleared his throat, pulled up his britches, and headed toward the group.

"Sheriff Wheeler," Adam said. "Sir, what are you doing here?"

"Just here to take a quick look around," came Wheeler's gruff voice as he pulled Adam away from the group.

Sarah handed Rugby's leash to her cousin. "Here. Take Rugby."

Emma took the leash. "What are you doing?"

Sarah hushed her cousin. "Trust me." She jogged up behind the two men and slowed her pace once she was close enough, following them as they walked toward Officer Finley.

"What are we looking at?" Wheeler asked.

Adam shook his head. "Not sure yet, sir."

They approached Officer Finley, who was still taking pictures from various angles of the rocks and of Rufus's body.

"See anything odd?" Wheeler asked Finley.

Officer Finley looked up from what he was doing. His light brown hair was cut short and combed back, though occasionally, pieces fell out of place, making him look even younger than he already was. "Looks like an accident. These rocks get pretty slick, especially at night when the tide comes in closer. Very easy to slip and bang your head pretty good."

"Uh, may I suggest…" Sarah started.

Sheriff Wheeler whipped his head around and gave Sarah a sharp gaze. "Sarah Shores. You shouldn't be out here."

"Well, sir," Adam said. "She heard Judy scream and made the call."

"Oh," Wheeler grumbled.

Sarah climbed closer to them. "May I say, sir, you look good without the beard."

"Oh?" Wheeler said, touching his bare cheek with his hand.

Sarah smiled. "Sheds decades off your face."

Wheeler gave her a slight smile, obviously flattered. "Well, thank you."

"Anyway, I don't think this was an accident," Sarah continued.

"Now what makes you say that, Miss Shores?"

Sarah pointed to the body. "When I got here, the body

was lying faceup, but Judy said that when she found her husband, she didn't know it was him until she turned him over, which suggests that he'd been on his side or stomach."

"Yeah, so?"

"So, the wound is on the back of his head. If he slipped and fell, hitting his head on the rocks, he would have been found lying on his back—faceup."

"What are you saying?"

"I'm saying, I think someone had moved the body."

"Hm." Wheeler rubbed his chin, then pointed to a gold ring with a green emerald on the victim's left hand. "Motivation for the murder doesn't seem to be a robbery."

Obviously, Sarah thought.

Wheeler returned his gaze to her. "Are you sure Mrs. Hattingsford said that this is how she found her husband?"

"Positive," Sarah said. "It's what she told me before Adam and Officer Finley arrived, and what she just told Adam."

Adam flipped through his notepad, then stopped on a particular page, reading. "Yeah, she's right. That's what she told me, too."

Sheriff Wheeler glanced at the body and then bent down, turning the victim's head slightly to one side to look at the wound. Then he stood. "We need another murder at Cascade Cove like I need another donut." He patted his round belly. Then he shook his head in disbelief. "Okay, let's do a search around the perimeter—see if we can find any more clues." He turned to Adam. "Dunkin, call for back up to help with the search. I want every inch of this area thoroughly combed, including behind the Hattingsfords' house."

"I'm on it, Sheriff," Adam said.

Sarah crouched down to take another close look at the victim, when the sheriff said, "Sarah, you should go back to the others. We'll take it from here."

Sarah got up and nodded—she didn't want to press her luck. He'd already listened to her, and it was known that Sheriff Wheeler didn't always heed others. He had pride. But one thing she knew for certain was that she'd built some credibility after helping solve the last three murders in Cascade Cove. Even if he didn't outwardly admit it, Wheeler seemed to trust her.

Sarah made her way back to her cousin, rather than pushing her luck by roaming around the "crime scene." She told her cousin what she had told the sheriff in private, away from the sisters and Buster, who was watching the men as they combed the area some more.

Within minutes, more cars and SUVs pulled up, and

a woman from the department was rolling out the crime scene tape.

Judy and Faith approached Sarah. "What is going on?" Judy asked. "I thought they said it was an accident?"

Sarah looked at her cousin, who was still standing in the same spot where she had left her with the two dogs. Before Sarah could answer Faith, Adam joined her and said, "Judy, I need to ask you and your sister a few more questions."

Faith crossed her arms. "I have a few questions of my own. Like, what is with the crime scene tape?"

Adam waved Buster over, ignoring Faith's question. He turned to Judy. "So, you said your husband went for a walk last night and you went to bed?"

Judy glanced at her sister quickly before nodding. "Yes, that's correct."

"And what time did you go to bed last night?"

"Uh, I'd say around 11 p.m."

Adam stopped writing and looked up from his pad. "You said your husband went for a walk and you went to bed right after he left?"

Judy nodded.

"Does your husband typically take late-night walks like that?"

"Sometimes."

"Did you two have an argument or anything?"

"No," Judy said.

Faith furrowed her eyebrows. "Are you trying to insinuate that my sister killed her husband?"

Judy faced her sister. "Faith!"

"No, ma'am," Adam said. "Just want to make sure that we get all the information."

Judy patted her sister on the shoulder. "Let them do their job."

Faith stared at Adam a moment longer. "Very well, but I'd like to say that she would never do such a thing. Especially to her husband."

"I understand, ma'am," Adam said. "And where were you last night?"

Faith lifted her chin slightly, not breaking eye contact with the officer. "I was in bed, asleep by nine-thirty," Faith said. "Unlike my sister, I like to go to bed at a more reasonable hour. I'm an early bird."

"And you didn't notice Mr. Hattingsford was missing?"

"Heavens, no!" Faith said, her voice an octave higher. "I assumed he was in bed. He usually doesn't get up until 9 a.m. It was well before eight when my sister discovered he was even missing."

"And you didn't help her search for him?"

"I just assumed he was out for a walk or something."

"But you just said he doesn't get up that early."

"No, but we all have off days."

Adam nodded. "Did either of you see or hear anything suspicious last night?"

Both women exchanged glances and shook their heads. Then Faith's face lit up. "I did hear Houdini barking last night."

Adam looked up from his pad, confused. "Houdini?"

"Yes," Faith said. "He's our dog, a Jack Russell."

"And at what time did you hear Houdini barking?"

Faith thought for a moment. "It was five of twelve. I remember because I looked at the time."

Adam was writing feverishly at this point. "Does he normally bark at night?"

"No, but I assumed that maybe he had seen a seagull or something, since we're in an area that he's unfamiliar with."

Adam turned to Buster. "How about you?"

"Me?" Buster asked. He was twirling a thick gold ring that had a gorgeous emerald-green stone on his right ring finger. "I was at the bar last night."

"Which bar?"

"Uh..." Buster shifted his eyes upward a moment, thinking.

Adam stopped writing and waited for a response.

Finally, Buster said, "I don't remember the name. It's a new bar. Wasn't here last year."

He thought a moment longer. "It's a tiki bar. Blond bartender, very muscular and very tanned."

Sarah recognized a small tinge of jealousy on Adam's face as the man described Teek.

"Teek's Tiki Bar?" Adam asked, looking down at his pad and avoiding eye contact.

Buster's face lit up with recognition of the name. "Yeah, that's it. I was there until about midnight, I'd say."

"So, witnesses saw you there at 12 a.m.?"

"I suppose."

"Okay," Adam said, giving his pen a quick click and flipping his notepad closed. "We'll be stopping by at the bar to see if anyone can corroborate your story."

Faith stepped toward Adam. "Say, now, what's this all about? Buster is Rufus's brother. This was clearly an accident."

"You seem really sure about that, Ms. Hartlob," Adam said. "Maybe you know more than you're letting on."

Faith's eyes went wide. "How dare you? None of us would kill Rufus. You're all insane, if that's what you're thinking."

"Well, Ms. Hartlob, I don't know about anyone's sanity, but of what I do know, you weren't too fond of Rufus."

Faith jabbed her fists into her hips. "Reading tabloids, I see."

Adam raised an eyebrow. "Usually, there's some truth in them."

"Well, I promise you, sir, you and your little minions won't find anything. None of us killed Rufus Hattingsford."

"Hey, guys!" Officer Finley called out from about ten feet below where Rufus's body lay motionless. "I think I found something!"

Adam and Sarah rushed toward Finley. She could hear Sheriff Wheeler yelling from the other side of the rocky terrain, "Miss Shores, you are not authorized to be here," but she ignored him, picking up her pace to see what Officer Finley had found. When she got there, she was confused—she didn't see anything.

"What is it?" Adam asked, anxiously looking around.

"There." Finley pointed to a rock the size of a small melon, lying on the ground. Adam and Sarah moved next to Finley to figure out what he was pointing at.

Sarah put her hand up to her mouth in shock. "Is that blood?"

CHAPTER 6

Sheriff Wheeler wheezed, and sweat rolled from his forehead. He took a hankie out from his pocket to dab away the perspiration. He had just jogged about thirty feet from where he'd been, and he was clearly feeling the effects of being out of shape—and past his prime. "What do we got?"

Officer Finley pointed to the blood-soaked rock.

Wheeler squatted down to take a better look. "Well, well. Seems like we just found ourselves the murder weapon." He stood slowly and with a great deal of effort. "Bag it and take it in."

Officer Finley crinkled his forehead. "Do we have a big enough bag?"

"Find one," Wheeler said. Then he turned to Sarah. "I suggest you and your cousin take off."

"But—" Sarah started.

Wheeler put up a hand, stopping her. "There's nothing more to see." He waved her away.

Adam turned to her and said, "I'll talk to you tonight." Then he lowered his voice to a whisper. "I'll let you know if we find anything else."

Sarah nodded and started making her way back up toward her cousin, who was straining to keep Rugby back.

"What is up with him?" Sarah asked.

"I don't know," Emma replied. "But I can't get him to relax. I think he wants to say hi to Adam."

"Maybe it's best if we just take him home before he gets loose. I'm sure Sheriff Wheeler won't be too happy if he ends up in the crime scene."

Sarah grabbed Rugby's lead from Emma and pulled him back. She glanced back at the scene, watching the sheriff and a handful of officers comb the area. She couldn't help but think of the poor residents of the Cove, and the vacationers who frequented the beachside town, who had had to cope with the ordeal of a washed-up landowner, a strangled food critic, and a shot artist, and now, they had to deal with the aftermath of a clubbed magician. Sure, the man had been quite abrasive, and in Sarah's short time being in his presence, the cranky man had insulted a poor woman and her young son, but no level of inconsideration was worthy of this. It was unlikely the woman had been the one to murder Rufus.

And there was Buster, who had been living in his brother's shadow. What if he had clubbed his brother out of jealousy? Or revenge?

"Ready to head back?" Emma said, interrupting Sarah's thoughts.

Sarah gave her cousin a brief smile. "Yeah, we should get back. It's getting late, and Grandpa is going to wonder where we are."

They headed toward the ramp that led back to the boardwalk. There was a crowd of people that had formed, curious about what was going on. An elderly woman with a purse the size of a suitcase touched Sarah's arm. "Excuse me, young lady," she said, her ocean-blue eyes filled with concern. "Do you know what's going on?"

Sarah stopped. She didn't want to botch the investigation, and she certainly didn't want to give out the wrong information to anyone in the public. Especially with how rumors spread in Cascade Cove. She didn't want to stoke the rumor mill. "Uh, I'm not in a position to talk about it."

"We, the people of Cascade Cove, should know

what's going on in our community," the woman demanded.

Sarah gave the woman an understanding nod. "I wish I could give you information, but I'm afraid—"

The woman's grip on Sarah's arm grew tighter, and she gave her an angry scowl. "We have a right to know!"

Sarah ripped her arm out from the woman's death grip as the woman shouted, "Bah!" in frustration. As Sarah turned to catch up to her cousin, she bumped straight into a tall man in a flat cap and a suit—the same man she'd seen at Patricia's Tea Room and on the street the day Rufus had left the boutique.

"Pardon me," he said, without looking at her. But Sarah could see his smooth face and hazel eyes shifting, bouncing from one thing to the next. He seemed preoccupied with the goings on behind the Hattingsfords' vacation home and was trying to weave through the crowd.

"Sarah!" She heard Emma's voice over the murmurs of the crowd and turned toward her cousin, who was already at the top of the ramp, on the boardwalk. Emma was waving to her, Winston at her feet.

Sarah pointed to the guy she'd just bumped into, but Emma shook her head, confused about what Sarah was trying to tell her.

Sarah whipped her head around, only to find the

man gone. Confused, she looked to her left, scanning the people in the crowd, and then to her right. But he was nowhere in sight. She could only hear the elderly woman repeat, "We have a right to know!"

When they walked into the shop, Larry was on the phone while simultaneously ringing out a line of customers. Emma quickly unhooked Winston's leash and rushed over to the register to take over for their grandpa.

"Surely. We can have it shipped to you before Christmas," Larry said into the phone. "Absolutely, ma'am. We can also have it gift wrapped." After one last pause, he said, "Thank you. That is much appreciated." He hung up the phone.

After the last customer Emma had rung up walked out the door, Larry turned to his two granddaughters. "Where on green Earth were you two? I think the Christmas rush has already started."

"Grandpa," Emma said, but Sarah reached out toward her cousin, pulling her back. She knew Emma too well. She was very straightforward. No, she was more than that. To put it plainly, she was blunt—too blunt sometimes.

Sarah stepped forward. "Grandpa," she said, voice sympathetic and gentle. "I think you should sit down."

Larry furrowed his brows. "Sit down? Good grief. What in tarnation is going on? You girls are always here in time for the store to open."

"I hate to be the one who has to tell you, but—" Sarah started.

The bells above the door jingled. "Howdy, everyone!" Mark's cheerful voice permeated the tension. He was carrying a package under one arm and his handy electronic device he used to scan the box in the other. He looked around at the lights and Christmas tree. "I love what you did with the place." Then he turned toward the two ladies and their grandfather. "I have a package for you all."

Mark Marino was Emma's first serious boyfriend since...well, forever. Sarah couldn't remember her cousin in any serious relationship before him. In fact, her cousin was very independent and usually scared men off with her sarcasm and no-nonsense attitude. She was never one to flirt—that is, until Mark came along. He was the only man Sarah had known to come across Emma's path that could not only take her sarcasm, but one-up her every time, and that made her cousin swoon, for some odd reason.

Emma immediately softened at Mark's pearly white

grin. "I didn't expect the bandana order to come for another three days. Boy, they are getting these orders delivered quick!" Emma put out her hand to take the electronic device so she could sign it.

Mark pulled the device back away from Emma. "Grabby today, aren't we? I hate to be the bearer of bad news, Em, but this is for Mr. Shores." He turned to Larry and handed him the stylus pen.

Larry's eyes sparkled with excitement. "This is a special order," he said, taking the stylus pen and signing for the package. He returned the pen to Mark and accepted the box. "It's for a magic trick I'm working on."

Emma nudged Sarah and said, "Told you."

Sarah chuckled. "What is it?" she asked Larry.

Larry grabbed a box cutter to open the package. "You'll see."

Emma shook her head before regarding her boyfriend. "So, Mark, I was wondering if you'd like to join us for Christmas dinner this year?"

"Wish I could," Mark said, "but I already promised my ma I'd spend Christmas with her and the family in Long Island."

Emma flapped her hand at him dismissively. "Oh, that's okay. I was just asking because I know your family doesn't live around here. I didn't want you to be alone."

"It's okay, really," Mark said. "The Marino family Christmas is cursed."

Sarah chuckled. "I'm sure that's not true."

"No, really," Mark said. "Every year, something absurd happens that ends the festivities early. Last year, it was the fight between my cousin Benny and Uncle Vinny. Benny tore Vinny's toupee off and threw it into Aunt Marci's cannoli dip. She cried while Benny and Vinny rolled around on the dinner table. Broke my ma's dishes. She was so mad. She grabbed the broom and tried to pry them off each other." Mark shook his head at the ridiculousness of his own family. "She threw them out, but their fight continued in the front lawn, attracting neighbors. Aunt Marci followed them and tried spraying them with the hose, but she couldn't break them up until the police arrived. Ma was so embarrassed."

"Oh, my," Emma said, her forehead creased in disbelief.

Mark shrugged. "Typical Marino reunion. I'm so used to it that now I make sure to bring popcorn."

Larry's ruffling through the package he'd just received drew everyone's attention. He pulled something out and unwrapped it. Then he set the box down and retrieved something from behind the counter, grin fixed to his face.

Mark eyed him. "Larry, what are you up to?"

Larry pulled out what appeared to be a deck of cards. "I have a special trick I've been working on." He took a single card from the pack, then turned so his back faced them, and struggled with something for a moment, before returning to where Sarah, Emma, and Mark waited.

"Okay," Larry said, holding up the single card. "It's just an ordinary playing card. Nothing special about it." He turned it so they could see that it was, indeed, a regular card—a queen of hearts, to be exact. "Now, as you can see, this hand is empty"—he showed them both sides of his left hand, then grabbed the card with that hand—"and my right hand is empty as well." He repeated the same motion, revealing both sides of his right hand.

Then he held out his right hand in front of him, palm facing the floor. Using his left hand, he made careful work of placing the card on the back of his flattened hand, so that they could all see the queen of hearts displayed. He slowly let go of the card, and it stood straight up as if it were balancing perfectly on its own.

"Ta da!" Larry said.

"Woah" and "wow" were the two words Sarah and Mark used to describe Larry's trick.

Then, the tags of two collars jingled, and both

Rugby and Winston swept past Larry's legs, jostling him slightly. His right hand quaked, and the card tumbled to the ground, along with some skin-colored object.

"What is that?" Sarah asked, pointing at the object.

Before Larry could crouch down to grab it, Rugby returned and gobbled the item up.

"Rugby!" Larry called out.

The yellow lab hurried away and was quickly out of sight, and Sarah could see Larry's face turning beet red. "That was my last one," he said.

"Your last what?" Emma asked.

"Magic thumb tip," Larry said, clearly disappointed.

Sarah raised an eyebrow. "Magic what?"

Larry sighed. "My magic thumb tip. It's a rubber, flesh-toned piece we magicians use to place over our thumbs to help us do our tricks."

"Let me see if I got this now," Emma said. "You used the thumb tip to balance the card on your hand by placing it behind the card?"

Sarah laughed. "That's why you had your back turned to us. You were fiddling with that thumb tip."

Larry grinned and threw his hands up. "You guys got me," he said with a chuckle. "I put the thumb tip on my thumb at the start of the trick. Once you picked your card and I showed you that I had nothing in my hands, I slipped the tip off, using it to prop up the card to make it look like it was standing on its own."

Sarah shook her head in amusement and wagged her finger at him. "You almost got us there. And I'll buy you a new set of magic thumb tips, Grandpa."

"Don't worry," Larry said. "I have more magic tricks I'm working on. You'll see!"

"Speaking of magic tricks," Mark said, "I just heard that something's going down over by Rufus's beach house."

Larry's eyes went wide. "Really? What?"

Both Emma and Sarah began talking over each other. "We should give them their privacy," Sarah said.

Emma flapped her hand. "I'm sure it's nothing. Rumors."

But it was too late—Mark had already spilled the beans. "I think they found Rufus's body by the Beachside Beacon, among the rocky terrain. They're saying he was murdered."

Larry gasped. "No! Not Rufus the Magnificent!"

After closing shop and having take-out for dinner from Fugimoto's Sushi Bar, Larry had closed himself off in his room, while Emma and Sarah were in the living room.

Sarah was knitting a large turtleneck sweater for a medium-sized dog, a special online order that had a quickly approaching deadline. She checked her phone again—no calls nor messages.

Sprawled out on the couch like a tossed rag doll, Emma was flipping through the channels on the TV.

Sarah huffed after Emma turned the channel for the umpteenth time. "Will you pick something?"

Emma sighed. "I'm sorry. I'm just worried about Grandpa. I haven't seen him this upset since his best friend passed away over ten years ago. He barely ate dinner, and he loves Fugimoto's Lobster Cove Roll Special. I know he always looked forward to seeing Rufus every year, but I didn't think he would be this upset."

It was heartbreaking to see their grandfather not act like his spunky self. After he'd found out that his favorite magician had not only died but was possibly murdered, he retreated within himself and had been quiet for the rest of the day. After dinner, he said he was going to bed. That was almost two hours ago.

Sarah put her knitting needles down. "He'll be okay. He just needs time. Grandpa always bounces back."

"You're right." Emma set the remote control on the coffee table and got up, stretching. "Maybe I should just call it a night."

"But it's not even nine."

"I know. Maybe I'll finish reading my book. Wasn't Adam supposed to call you or something to let you know what they've learned about Rufus?"

Sarah sighed. "Haven't heard anything yet."

"I'm sure Adam's just busy."

Sarah nodded as Emma headed back to her room.

After another hour of knitting, lightning in the window caught Sarah's attention. She checked her phone again. Nothing.

Getting up, Sarah headed to the bedroom that she and her cousin shared. Emma still had her nightstand light on, and the yellow glow illuminated the room enough that Sarah could see just fine. She walked over to her cousin, who had her book open facedown on her chest and was lightly snoring.

Sarah picked up the book, placing her thumb between the two pages Emma had it open to so she didn't lose her place and found the book marker lying next to her. Placing the bookmark in the pages, she gently set the book on her cousin's nightstand and pulled the covers up to her cousin's chin. Emma mumbled in her sleep and rolled onto her side.

Ambling to the dresser drawers, Sarah changed into her pajamas, then shuffled into the bathroom to wash her face and brush her teeth, before turning out all the lights and crawling under her own covers.

Lying there, she thought about Rufus, the crime scene, Judy and Faith. Then Buster came to mind. But what person would want to kill their own brother? Though, it was definitely a possibility. Then her mind wandered to the mother with her little boy. She hadn't given much thought to the woman whom Rufus had berated, though it was hard to believe a mother would do such a thing. Maybe the woman had told her husband, and he'd wanted to get even. No. Sarah shook the thoughts away. She had to get some sleep, and thinking about all of this would keep her up.

Closing her eyes, she tried to think about the beach, the sand and waves, the salty air. A flock of seagulls swooped overhead, squawking. Feeling the tiny grains of sand trickle between her toes, she plodded toward the water. The birds up above her screeched as if they were in a squabble. Sarah tilted her head back and was surprised to see only one white bird soar deeper into the blue sky, before charging straight toward her like a torpedo. It was only inches from her face when it honked, jolting her instantly back into the dark reality where she lay safe in her bed.

When she'd awakened, she realized it wasn't a terrifying seagull after her. It was her phone that had buzzed, alerting her a message had been received. She picked it up—who would be texting her at this hour? She squinted against the harsh blue light of the screen—it was a message from Adam. *Sarah, we found something. Meet me tomorrow at Patricia's Tea Room at 5 p.m.*

The room lit up brightly as another flash of lightning threatened the sky, blinding her, followed by a loud rumble of thunder. She wondered if she'd get any sleep tonight.

CHAPTER 7

Sarah woke to a white, round tuft of fur rising and falling right in front of her face.

"Ugh, Winston!" Sarah said as she pulled herself away from the corgi's heart-shaped butt. The chubby corgi shuffled under the covers, backing up to reveal his comically big ears and tired face.

"What are you doing here?" she asked, though with the thunderstorm last night, she wasn't surprised to find him in her bed. Even the rolling thunder that could barely be heard in the distance still frightened the poor thing, and she'd often find him nuzzled as close to her as possible. He'd even climbed on top of her, pushing the air out of her body and causing her to let out an *oomph* sound. He wasn't exactly a teacup puppy, yet she welcomed him and had gone as far as buying doggy steps so that he could crawl into bed with her when he wanted to. Otherwise, he would whine in the middle of the night, waking her. Mostly, though, he would sleep in his comfy foam bed with his night-night blanket.

She rubbed under his chin, and that's when she noticed the sweet aroma of maple and sausage. Reaching for her phone, she checked the time—7:30 a.m.

"Wonder who's cooking breakfast," Sarah said to Winston.

In response, the corgi let out a big yawn, and Sarah threw the covers off and slipped into her fuzzy pink robe and slippers that she had brought with her from New York. A little overkill for a Florida morning, but it was all she had for the time being. She padded out of her room and down the hall into the kitchen, to find Grandpa Larry flipping a pancake.

Sarah rubbed her eyes.

Larry was wearing a white cooking apron with a big red lobster on the front baring chomping claws; the apron read, "Don't Mess with the Cook."

"Good morning," he said with a smile.

Emma was already at the table, stuffing a sausage log down her gullet.

"Grandpa," Sarah said. "Are you okay?"

Larry turned to her, spatula in hand. "Hm?" He was obviously preoccupied. A buzzer sounded, and Larry rushed over to the egg timer to shut it off. He opened the oven, and the smell of oranges and spice filled the room. Larry eyed whatever it was he had in there and furrowed his eyebrows. "Not quite done yet," he said, closing the oven door.

"What's in there?" Sarah asked.

Larry cranked the old white timer and placed it back on the counter. "Figured you were missing fall days in New York, and so I thought I'd try my hand at baking these maple spiced orange muffins. Get it? It's autumn spice meets Florida oranges."

Now Sarah knew something wasn't right. Not that it was uncommon for Larry to make breakfast or any other meal—he loved to cook, but baking was a whole other matter. He was a disaster with anything that involved flour and butter.

"Are you feeling all right, Grandpa?" Sarah asked.

Larry flipped a pancake over and began turning the sausages one by one in the other pan. "I feel fine. Why?"

Sarah's brows rippled in confusion. After a long evening of her Grandpa moping around over the famous magician's death, it was hard to believe he'd be over it so quickly, as if it had never happened. "I thought you would still be grieving over…you know…" Sarah was afraid to say the magician's name in case it triggered her grandfather.

"Rufus?" Larry asked, completing her sentence. "There's no point in dwelling for too long. I'll keep his memory alive by learning more magic tricks." Then he looked up. "Hey, I have an idea. Maybe I can put on a magic show of my own!"

Sarah scratched her head and looked at her cousin for some sort of explanation or answer to Larry's behavior, but Emma only gave a shrug and shoveled the rest of her sausage into her mouth.

"I don't know, Grandpa," Emma said, wiping the grease from the corners of her mouth with a napkin. "Magicians work for years on their tricks to make them believable."

"Bah," Larry said without looking at her. "It doesn't take that long, unless you're working on a massive trick like making the Statue of Liberty disappear. Maybe I could find some white doves," he said, a finger to his chin.

Emma shook her head. "The last thing we need right now are doves in the boutique."

"You're right." Larry tapped his finger against his chin a few times. "They'd probably leave droppings during a trick." Larry thought a moment longer, before his eyes grew wide with excitement. "Oh, how about a rabbit?"

Sarah sighed. All she could think about was how Misty would react to a bunny hopping around the store.

"I don't know, Grandpa," Sarah said. "Maybe you should try something smaller."

Larry nodded. "You're right. I'll need time to think about it. Besides, doves and rabbits are so cliché." He grabbed the white-and-yellow striped hand towel he had resting on his shoulder and used it to grip the handle of the hot skillet. "Sarah," he said, "why don't you join Emma at the table? The food is almost ready."

Sarah took her seat next to her cousin, where there was already a plate and silverware waiting for her. Her grandfather made his way to the table with a tall stack of oddly shaped pancakes. It looked as though he had cooked them at various temperatures. Some were burnt and others seemed a tad undercooked.

"Pick your pancake," he said, spatula ready. Sarah pointed at the two that seemed the most edible. He shoveled them onto her plate before offering Emma her flat cakes.

"So, you know who did it?" he asked.

Sarah was drizzling syrup onto her breakfast. "Me?"

"Well, you are the Jessica Fletcher of the family."

"No, I think that's Grandma," Sarah said. Grandma Ruth, who worked on a cruise ship for most of the year, was no stranger to murder and mystery. She was a no-nonsense, sweet, and observant lady who had a knack for fashion—a trait neither Sarah nor Emma had inherited. But when Grandma was home, Sarah spent many days with her either in the kitchen learning how to bake her amazing cakes and desserts or helping her cut out articles and pictures for her many scrapbooks.

"I'd say Sarah is more like the Nancy Drew of the family," Emma said, loading her fork with buttery pancakes and somehow managing to wedge it all in her mouth. It was beyond Sarah how her cousin consistently maintained her slender figure while Sarah herself had to run ten miles to work off a single cookie.

"Either way," Larry said. "I'm sure Sarah has an idea. We need to get to the bottom of this. We can't let the person who did this to the wonderful Rufus get away with it."

At her Grandpa's words, Sarah filled her mouth with some pancakes herself. She didn't want to be the one to break it to him that the magician was actually a rude, brash man, and it seemed like Emma was riding that same boat. It was probably for the best.

"I don't know," Sarah said.

"What do you mean, you don't know?" Larry asked. "What about his family? You met his family, right?"

Sarah nodded.

Larry shifted his weight. “Maybe it was a friend? I mean, who could possibly want a brilliant man like Rufus dead?”

Sarah could think of a few people. Mainly, the mother who had come in with her boy the day before. Though, she didn’t exactly suspect the mother of foul play. She was an author of children’s books. It could have been the father, but that was even more far-fetched to Sarah.

The timer buzzed again. “The muffins,” Larry said, getting up from his chair and heading into the kitchen. “What about his wife?” Larry asked from the kitchen.

Sarah sawed through one of the sausages on her plate. “It could have been her. The spouse is usually the first to be questioned.”

“Or maybe it was his brother, Buster. Remember, he was living in his brother’s shadow all these years. He could have gotten fed up and bumped him over the head with a rock.”

“I’ll know more once I talk to Adam tonight,” Sarah said.

“So, he finally contacted you last night?”

“Yeah, and it was late. I was already falling asleep when I got the text message.”

Larry walked in with a couple of the maple spiced orange muffins on a plate. He dumped one muffin onto

Sarah's plate, and it fell over and rolled toward her pancakes. Sarah raised an eyebrow at her grandfather, who was smiling with pride as he took his seat again. Based on the incredible bounce of the muffins, it was clear they weren't going to be moist. Hopefully, she wouldn't damage a tooth or anything. Picking up the muffin, she said a small prayer before taking a bite. It was like biting into a rubber duck. She chewed deliberately, giving Larry a thumbs up. She grabbed her glass of orange juice to wash it down.

"So, what did the message say?" Emma asked, shoving her own muffin aside, away from her pancakes. "Did he give you any clues, Sarah?"

"He just said that they'd found something."

Emma's face lit up in excitement. "I wonder what it is."

"Hopefully something that will lead you right to the killer," Larry said. "They could skip town and get away with it."

"Grandpa's right," Emma said. "They'll be harder to catch if they skip town."

"True," Sarah said, "but even if they do leave the area, we can still catch them."

"If you haven't noticed, we have a fairly small police department here in Cascade Cove," Emma said. "It's not like New York, where they have all the forensic stuff."

Her cousin was right, but Sarah was confident they'd figure it out. They had done so three times before. How hard could it be to solve a fourth mystery?

CHAPTER 8

After helping her grandfather clean up the disaster he had made in the kitchen, and getting herself washed up and ready for the day, Sarah stumbled into the boutique to find her cousin talking with a large man Sarah didn't recognize. When Emma caught sight of her, she waved her over. "Sarah, come here. I want you to meet someone."

Sarah walked over to them, smile on her face.

"This is my cousin I was telling you about," Emma was saying to the huge man.

He turned to Sarah and held out his thick hand. "Hi, I'm Atticus Detweiler."

Sarah lost her hand in his massive paw, but still gave him a firm handshake. "I'm Sarah. Nice to meet you Mr. Detweiler."

"You can call me Atticus."

Emma leaned over the counter toward Sarah and jabbed a thumb in the man's direction. "He used to be Rufus's manager."

The man chuckled. "More like his secretary. I booked the shows and took his phone calls, but that was years ago. Until the ungrateful man fired me."

"Oh, no," Sarah said. "What for?"

"For not taking care of his 'problem,'" Atticus said, using quotation fingers while stating the word, "problem." Atticus leaned in closer to Sarah and continued, "'Problem' meaning his brother, Buster. He wanted me to take him out."

Sarah's eyes went wide. It wasn't difficult to imagine what a big fellow like Atticus could do to a spindly magician like Buster. She swallowed hard. "Take him out?"

"Oh." The gorilla of a man chuckled. "Not like that. No, I'm talking sabotage."

Sarah furrowed her brows. "What do you mean?"

"Buster was quickly becoming a well-known magician. He saw this as a wonderful break for himself and his brother, who was already well established in the magician world. He'd even thought about putting together an act with Rufus. But Rufus saw his brother as more of a competitor than a partner. So, he called on me to take care of him."

"And when you say, 'take care of him,' you mean?"

"I mean, sabotage his big act. See, Buster was doing a show in New York at the Grand Arena. We're talking big-time. The kind of show that could make or break you. Buster was prepared to do one of his famous tricks that got his name out there. An escape act where he would transport himself from a glass box, trading places with his assistant. Rufus offered me twenty-five grand to make sure the curtain he used malfunctioned, revealing the secret to the trick on national television. When I refused, he fired me."

Sarah shook her head in disbelief. "His own brother?"

"I'm surprised you haven't heard of Buster's fifteen minutes of fame. Though, judging by your age, you're probably too young to remember." He smiled. Then he held up a finger. "Ah," he said, digging in his pocket. "I'll show you!" He pulled out his cell phone, swiping and tapping the screen. Then he laid the phone on the counter, screen up, and they circled around the device. He'd found the footage on VideoTube, entitled, *The Magician, Buster, is a Bust!* Atticus hit the play button.

A young man with red hair and freckles, who appeared

to be in his early twenties, was sitting in front of his camera. He smiled before he spoke: "Buster the Brilliant was an up-and-coming magician following in his brother's footsteps, the glorious Rufus the Magnificent. But Buster turned out to be a bust when he decided to perform an act that discredited him as a brilliant magician."

The video transitioned into a flashy intro with music, and eventually, a title appeared on the screen in bright red: *Timothy Tells It All.* Then the video transitioned back to the young man. "Thanks for tuning in to Timothy Tells It All. I'm Timothy, and in this video, I'm going to show you an act that was aired on national TV, where a magician named 'Buster the Brilliant' is shown trying to perform a teleportation act using what looks like a glass box. Ever hear of this magician? Neither have I, and now I can show you why, in this hilarious magic trick fail. Let's take a look!"

The video transformed into a grainy video that Sarah could only assume was made in the nineties. On screen was Buster, who wore a loose white button-down shirt and a pair of form-fitted dark slacks. His assistant, on the other hand, was sporting a flashy red dress, stiletto heels, and fishnet stockings that showed off her slim thighs.

"His assistant is really pretty," Emma said.

"Of course, she's pretty," Atticus said. "Magician's

always make sure to have a beautiful assistant. It's half the show." He gave her a wink.

They focused their attention back on Atticus's phone screen. It showed Buster climbing up a ladder, into a glass box that sat on top of a pillar and platform. His assistant closed the box and removed the ladder, while Buster banged on the walls, showing it was sturdy. His assistant grabbed a curtain hanging over the side of the box and pulled it over the box to cover it. She unfolded another curtain to cover herself, but not before showing off a brilliantly white smile before disappearing behind the curtain. Within seconds, Buster was in the place of his assistant, and the curtain fell, revealing his assistant climbing up a ladder to the box. Sarah could hear the audience laughing as Buster dropped his end of the curtain and gave a bow, unaware of what had just happened behind him.

"Oh!" Timothy shouted. "Did you see that? Let's play it in slow motion."

Again, the curtain fell, only this time very slowly, revealing once again the assistant climbing a ladder into the box.

The video panned onto Timothy's red face as he snorted back another laugh. When he was finished, he said, "Anyway, let me know in the comments below what you think of this doofus. And let me know if you have ever seen his brother, the real magician, Rufus the Magnificent. Next week, I'll be posting a video of an animal tamer that almost gets mauled to death by a lion! So, be sure to follow me so you don't miss it!"

Sarah's forehead crinkled at the thought of a person being mauled by an animal.

The screen went black, and Atticus picked his phone up from the counter, shutting it off and slipping it back into his pocket. "This act single-handedly destroyed Buster's reputation."

"And Rufus wanted you to sabotage his act?" Sarah asked.

"Obviously, I didn't. After I was fired, I saw this on live TV. I prayed everything would run smoothly for Buster. He isn't anything like Rufus. He's kind and generous. But you can imagine my horror when the curtain malfunctioned. I knew Rufus was behind it. Now, I hear years later that Rufus is not only dead but murdered!"

"How did you find out?" Sarah asked. "I don't think that it's public knowledge yet."

Atticus nodded. "Yes, it is. At least, in the magician community. It spread like wildfire. Emails, texts, videos —you name it. A small town like Cascade Cove couldn't cover up a massive story like the legendary Rufus the Magnificent, no matter how hard they tried."

Sarah sighed. "I guess not."

Atticus continued, "There's more."

Sarah cocked her head. "More?"

"I have my own suspicions. Very legit suspicions."

"Like what?" Sarah asked.

"Like, I told Buster what happened during his act, what Rufus had offered me to sabotage him, and why. I also made it clear to him that I turned it down, but that I didn't think it was an accident. His brother must've hired someone to do it." Atticus shifted his eyes to the floor.

Sarah stepped closer to the large man. "What is it, Atticus? What's on your mind?"

Atticus met Sarah's eyes—the shame and sadness behind them was clear as day.

Finally, Atticus spoke: "I had called Buster and finally told him about his brother's involvement in the curtain malfunction, and the downfall of his career...the day before Rufus was found dead."

CHAPTER 9

"Can you believe Buster's own brother would be capable of such a thing?" Emma asked. "What a heartless goon."

"No, Emma. I'm not surprised," Sarah said. "I mean, we witnessed it ourselves, how crass the man could be. I don't put it past him to sabotage his own brother."

Emma plopped down in her chair, allowing it to bounce and turn slightly to the left. "And to think, Buster could be behind his own brother's murder."

"We don't know that for sure."

"No, but the evidence certainly points toward his brother," Emma said.

Sarah shook her head. Her cousin still didn't get that hearsay was not evidence. "We don't know how credible

Atticus really is. And his presence is kind of strange, don't you think?"

Emma straightened herself. "Wait. You don't think Atticus himself had anything to do with Rufus's murder, do you?"

"I'm not saying that, but we do have to keep in mind that he was fired by a 'legendary' magician," Sarah said, being sure to use the same adjective as Rufus's ex-manager had used to describe the man.

Emma gasped. "You're right. I hadn't thought of that." Emma leaned back in her chair and shook her finger at her cousin. "You're good."

Sarah looked at the clock. "No, I'm just suspicious of everyone. I don't take everyone's word at face value. People spin the truth." She pulled her hair back, using the scrunchy that hung from her wrist.

"Uh-oh," Emma said. "Where are you going?"

She pulled the scrunchy tight, allowing her hair to hang freely from it. "I'm going to pay a visit to our friend, Teek. Buster claims that he was at the bar during his brother's murder. I just want to check it out. See if Teek remembers seeing him there at that time."

"Isn't Adam going to check with Teek?"

"Probably, but I can't wait while the police drag their feet." Sarah shrugged.

Emma arched an eyebrow.

"They're busy," Sarah said. "Let's just say I'm an understanding person who wants to help out." Sarah made her way to the door.

Emma regarded her cousin seriously. "Just make sure that Sheriff Wheeler doesn't catch wind of this, or you and Adam will be in trouble."

"Nonsense. He can't get mad at me for talking to a friend." Sarah winked before walking out the door.

A few minutes later, Sarah was in front of Teek's Tiki Bar. She tried the door. It was open, and she stepped into the first room. It was a speakeasy bar, and usually there was a man that sat at the table. But this time, the chair behind the table was empty, so she ignored the usual initiation of signing the guestbook. She'd signed it dozens of times in the past to go into Teek's bar, even if it was just for a minute.

Opening the curtain to the bar's entrance, she stepped inside. Wooden chairs were upside down on the tables that surrounded a small dance floor. Surfing music filled the room, and though the jukebox in the corner was lit, the music wasn't coming from it. Perhaps a small boombox was playing behind the bar.

The place was empty and dark, except for the several yellow lights that glowed dimly from the ceiling. There were also strings of lights that drooped down from the wall behind the bar. Though the lights were up all year round, it gave a Sarah a warm holiday feeling now that Christmas was just around the corner—or maybe it was the Santa in the opposite corner, wearing Bermuda shorts.

Behind the bar, she saw Teek with his unbrushed, sun-bleached hair tied back into a bun. He was wearing a snazzy, brightly colored vest with a cluttered pattern on it and a button-down shirt underneath, where he left a few of the top buttons undone, revealing his broad, tight chest. His biceps bulged as he rotated a wadded rag inside a glass mug.

He was an attractive guy; this did not escape Sarah by any means. She could understand Adam's jealousy toward her and Teek's friendship, especially after the one summer she'd spent with Teek after her junior year of high school. She'd thought Adam had stood her up at a beach party, only to learn a few months ago that he hadn't stood her up. That particular night, Adam had seen Sarah with Teek and thought he'd witnessed them kissing. But that wasn't what happened. Sarah had fallen while dancing with some friends, scraping her chin in the process, and Teek was only performing first aid. Under the impression Adam had stood her up, she had spent the rest of the summer learning how to surf with Teek.

But Teek wasn't her type. And as far as Sarah was concerned, it would be hard for any woman to make an honest man out of Teek anyway. He was carefree. Spontaneous. And the complete opposite of serious. Except when it came to surfing, of course.

"What's up, dudette?" Teek said, smiling. His perfectly aligned pearly whites were a nice contrast to his deeply tanned skin.

Sarah walked briskly to the bar and hopped up on one of the bar stools, her feet dangling slightly above the floor. Darn her short stature, a curse among the Shores gals. The Shores family was filled with only petite women. Cute, but certainly not tall, gorgeous models.

"I was wondering if I could ask you a question," Sarah said.

"Want a drink? We don't open for another half hour, but I can hook you up with something on tap. Got a lot of glasses to dry. You know, another crazy night last night." He chuckled.

"No, just the question."

"Okay, then. Shoot."

"I was wondering if you saw a man by the name of Buster here on Wednesday between the times 11:30 p.m. and midnight?"

"What does this Buster dude look like?"

"Oh, uh, he's tall. Kind of gangly. Thinning red hair…" Sarah was running out of descriptions.

Teek shook his head. "Hm… I'll need more than that. Lots of people come in and out of here."

Sarah sighed. Then she perked up. "Oh, he wears a massive gold ring with a green stone on his left middle finger."

Teek thought a moment. "Wait, Buster. Isn't he the magician's brother or something?"

"Yes!"

Teek nodded. "Yeah, I remember that dude. He also had on a mood ring that told the future or some crazy story."

"Really?" Sarah asked.

"Yeah, it was black, and he said that his night was bleak. That something unfortunate would happen in the near future, and he needed a drink."

Sarah's eyes went wide. "He said that?"

Teek laughed. "Don't tell me you believe that hocus pocus."

"His brother was murdered that night."

Teek's face transformed into realization, then shock. "Woah, that's right. Wow, I guess there might've been some truth in it, then. Bummer."

Sarah waved her hands in front of her. "Forget about

that. Was he here between 11:30 p.m. and midnight that night?"

Teek's eyes shifted toward the ceiling, and he scratched his head. "He was gone before twelve that night."

"Are you sure?"

"Yeah, I remember because Tara Huckleman plays that 'Sweet Home Alabama' song at quarter to midnight." Tara Huckleman was a middle-aged, bottle-blonde woman who teased her hair until it was a massive nest on top of her head. She wore globs of mascara and rouge and wore tight, skimpy outfits. Though, despite her age, she could certainly pull them off. She'd lost her husband in a fatal car accident several years back. Ever since Teek had opened his tiki bar, she had been a devoted patron who frequented the bar every single night. Though she was a handsy woman when she drank, persuading any man to dance with her throughout the night, she always paid honor to her late husband by playing "Sweet Home Alabama" at about the same time he was reported to have died.

"Tara was all over that Buster dude. Loved his story about the future-telling ring. He even pulled a red flower from behind her ear or something. Really grabbed her attention that night."

"I see." Sarah could only imagine how the flower

trick would have made Tara swoon. She also wondered how many times Buster had used that trick to attract women.

"Anyway, she made her typical rounds, saying hello to the other regulars, but once she'd punched in her song"—Teek motioned toward the brightly lit, red-and-yellow jukebox that sat snug in the back of the bar—"she was looking all over for him. She even asked me. I looked for him, but he was nowhere. Jerry Dunmeyer said he saw him leave ten minutes before. Said he was mad about his brother or something and was just at the bar to get away."

That would have been around 11:35 p.m., to be exact. That was, of course, if this Jerry guy had actually meant exactly ten minutes.

Sarah slapped the bar with her palm. "Thanks, Teek!" She got up off her stool, having to literally hop down.

"Are you leaving already?"

"Sorry, Teek," Sarah said, hoisting her purse onto her shoulder. "I have some work to do. I'll be back to catch up later."

Sarah started toward the door when Teek called out to her.

"Are you going to be at the annual Surfing Santas competition tomorrow?" he asked.

Sarah smiled. She'd almost forgotten, though she

knew Grandpa would make sure she was there. It was all he talked about, since the off-season had started. In fact, the big event was something everyone in town had been talking about. And from what she'd heard the past couple of months, her friend Teek never missed dressing up as Santa and surfing the waves, showing off his moves. "I wouldn't miss it for the world."

CHAPTER 10

Sarah hurried down the main strip, taking a turn toward the police station. She couldn't wait until their meeting at Patricia's Tea Room this evening to tell Adam what she had just discovered and, not to mention, learn what Adam had found. When she arrived at the station, she whipped the heavy glass door open and strolled in to find the pudgy Officer Deats at the front desk.

Officer Deats had been in the Cascade Cove Police Department since 1985. Though at one time young and lean, he had let himself go over the years just like his boss, Sheriff Wheeler. But, according to what she'd heard around town, the dimwitted Officer Deats had succumbed to an injury during an investigation that no one seemed too keen on talking about. Whatever had happened had landed Deats in the hospital for weeks and left him with much slower reflexes, even after physical therapy. But instead of taking leave or retiring early, he'd opted to take over at the front desk.

Sarah removed her sunglasses and approached him. His head was down while he seemed to be amusing himself with something on the desk, though Sarah couldn't see what it was because of a small barrier that surrounded the desk, covering it by six inches.

She stood there for a moment, waiting. Then she realized he was on his phone, watching some funny cat video—a cat wailed and people in the video laughed. Deats snickered, eyes still glued to his screen.

Sarah cleared her throat.

Deats looked up and jumped slightly at the sight of a person standing directly in front of him. After a moment, he said, "Cats. They're just so darn funny." Then he pushed the phone off to the side. "So, what can I help you with? Here to pay a fine? Because if you are, we no longer—"

Sarah shook her head. "No. I'm Sarah, remember? I need to see Officer Adam Dunkin right away."

"Oh, right," he said. "You're his girlfriend, Sarah."

"I'm not his girlfriend," she said, a little more sternly than she'd intended. It sounded defensive.

Deats looked up. "Right," he said, lifting his brows suspiciously. "Excuse me. *Not* his girlfriend."

Sarah sighed. "Could you please just tell him I'm here to see him?"

"Of course." He picked up the phone, tapped a few buttons, and said, "Dunkin, I have someone here to see you. A Sarah…uh…"

"Shores," Sarah said.

"Right, Sarah Shores, who's *not* your girlfriend," he said, stressing the word "not."

Sarah narrowed her eyes at Deats, but he kept his eyes aimed on something on his desk as he listened to Adam on the other end.

"Uh-huh…Uh-huh," Deats said. He looked at Sarah and said one last "uh-huh" into the receiver before hanging it up.

"What did he say?" Sarah asked. "Can I go back now?"

Deats was filling out a yellow card on his desk with a black pen. "He doesn't sound too happy about seeing you. He compared you to a hurricane."

"A hurricane? What's that supposed to mean?"

"I don't know, but he also seconds your motion about the whole girlfriend thing."

Sarah huffed, rolling her eyes. "He better."

Then he lifted his head, handing her what looked like

a pass. "Keep this on you in case you bump into Melinda. She'll ask to see it. They're tightening up security around here, and they want to make sure that all visitors who come through this threshold have checked in with me first." He puffed up his chest proudly, making his big belly bump stick out further.

"Sounds like a big job," Sarah said, taking the card.

"Yup, but someone's gotta do it," Deats said. "You know where room twelve is? Down the hall and to the left, third door on the right."

Sarah nodded.

"You can head back now," he said, pointing a pudgy thumb to a door behind him.

Sarah gave the man a curt nod and made her way through the door. She looked down the hall, not seeing anyone, including Melinda, though she wasn't quite sure who this Melinda woman was. Come to think of it, she didn't remember Adam ever talking about a Melinda.

Walking down the hall, she turned a corner, passing several more closed doors before arriving at room twelve.

She tapped on the door's glass window.

"Come in," Adam's voice boomed.

When Sarah opened the door, he was standing behind his desk, hands in his pockets. Not a good sign.

He only did that when he was upset, like sticking his hands in his pockets kept him from going berserk.

"Sarah, I told you I'd meet you at Patricia's tonight. You have any idea the amount of trouble I could get into if the sheriff finds out that I'm relaying this information to you?"

"No, I don't," Sarah said. "I don't even know what kind of information you have."

Adam let out a frustrated breath. He pulled his hand out of his pocket and combed his fingers through his thick, dark hair.

Sarah stepped closer. "And that's not why I came here in the first place."

Adam turned to her. "You're lucky the sheriff is out to lunch right now."

Sarah ignored him and took a seat in one of the chairs opposite his desk. "I wanted to stop by because *I* may have some information you'd probably like to know in regard to Rufus's murder."

Adam let out one final breath before taking a seat himself. He rested his arms on his desk in defeat. "What is it? What did you find?"

"I didn't find anything. A man stopped by at the shop. Claims to have known Rufus way back during the high-time of his career."

"His manager, Atticus Detweiler?"

"How'd you know?"

"We questioned him already. He told us he used to be his manager, and that he knew nothing about the murder."

Sarah's eyes went wide. "Don't you find it kind of an odd coincidence that he would be in Cascade Cove when Rufus—"

Adam put up his hand to stop her. "Sarah, he's here visiting his niece. He barely even knows Rufus's family, especially after all these years. There's no connection."

"Fine," Sarah said. "But did you know Buster was also a magician?"

Adam nodded. "We did extensive background checks on all those who were staying with Rufus that night."

"Oh, good," Sarah said. "So, you know why Buster's career didn't take off like his brother's?"

Adam leaned back in his chair. "Of course. He wasn't as good a magician as his brother. Those are some big shoes to fill."

Sarah waved his words away. "Yeah, yeah. Of course. But you know about his infamous act in New York that went national? The one where the curtain malfunctioned, revealing how Buster did the trick?"

"Yes, we know all about that. What does this have to do with anything, Sarah?"

Sarah frowned. "I'm getting to that." She could tell Adam was growing impatient. "Anyway, Atticus Detweiler was in the shop today. He told me that Rufus had asked him to sabotage his brother's magic act for a pretty penny, but when he refused, he fired Atticus on the spot."

"That's hear—"

"Hearsay," Sarah said, interrupting him. She smiled. "I thought you might say that."

"What are you smiling about?"

"Remember what Buster said yesterday when we found Rufus's body?"

Adam nodded his head. "About being at Teek's Tiki Bar the night before? He didn't say much."

Sarah knew he would remember. Especially since Buster had brought up Adam's arch nemesis since high school. "Right! And what time did he leave?"

Adam shuffled through some papers. He placed a finger on what he was looking for, gliding the finger across the page as he read. "He said he was there until about midnight, which would give him an alibi for his brother's murder." Adam looked up. "That is, if the murder took place during the time the dog, Houdini, started carrying on."

"Right again! So, I paid Teek a little visit—"

"Sarah! I told you that we were going to question

Teek. I don't need you coming in like a hurricane, messing—"

It was Sarah's turn to interrupt. "Teek distinctly remembers Buster leaving at 11:35 p.m."

Adam paused, his face relaxing. "He does?"

Sarah nodded with satisfaction.

"But how does Teek know he wasn't there at exactly 11:35 p.m.?"

"You know, typical regulars, playing songs at certain times every night."

"You mean, Tara Huckleman playing 'Sweet Home Alabama' at a quarter to midnight?"

Sarah wasn't surprised Adam knew about Tara's nightly tradition. Most of the locals knew about it. "Precisely," she said. "When she played the song that night, she was looking for Buster, who'd been flirting with her all night, but she couldn't find him. That's because he'd already left. Jerry Dunmeyer told Teek that Buster had left ten minutes before, stating that he was mad at his brother. That means he left at—"

"11:35 p.m.," Adam said, completing Sarah's sentence.

"Yes! Twenty minutes before his brother's murder. That would give him plenty of time to walk home, see his brother walking around the Beacon, and strike him in the back of the head with a melon-sized rock in a fit of rage at exactly 11:55 p.m." Sarah would have huffed hot air onto her finger nails and buffed them on her shirt, but she thought that would be too over the top, even for Adam. So, instead, she crossed her arms as smugly as she could muster while waiting for his response.

Adam took a deep breath, digesting everything Sarah had just said. "It's still a long shot, Sarah. Buster couldn't even pull off a magic trick. What makes you think he could pull off a murder?"

Sarah rolled her eyes. "That's only because someone sabotaged his act. Haven't you been listening? Besides, I didn't tell you the best part."

"Okay," Adam said, nestling back in his chair. "I'll humor you."

"Atticus said that he had just recently told Buster about his brother's plans to destroy his magician career the day before Rufus was found dead."

Adam chuckled. "You think you got this all figured out, don't you?"

"I think I do," she said, raising an eyebrow.

Adam shook his head before opening a drawer on his desk and pulling out a bag.

Sarah couldn't help but crane her neck to see what it was.

"You know what this is?" Adam asked, tossing the bag onto the table.

There was a big label on the bag that obscured Sarah's vision of what was inside. She picked it up.

"We found this at the crime scene after you left," Adam said. "It was clutched in Rufus's right hand."

Sarah picked up the bag and turned it over.

It was a red handkerchief.

CHAPTER 11

"Sarah? Are you okay?" Adam asked.

Sarah was speechless. Was it the same red handkerchief she had seen the strange man wearing in his front breast pocket at Patricia's Tea Room? There was no mistake. It was the same bright shade of red that clashed with the rest of his outfit. Yes, this was the same red handkerchief she'd seen on the man who had been roaming around Cascade Cove since Rufus's arrival, sticking out like a sore thumb.

"Sarah?" Adam said. His voice was louder this time, snapping her out of her trance. "What is going on?"

"I've seen this handkerchief before."

Adam perked up. "What? Are you sure?"

Sarah didn't tear her eyes away from the handkerchief. She couldn't. "Yeah. There was a strange man that came into Patricia's Tea Room the day we were there for the key lime bars."

"What did he look like?"

"Oh, I don't know." Sarah paused a moment. "I just noticed that he was dressed weird."

"Weird how?"

"He had on a tweed suit. Um, he caught my eye because the red handkerchief didn't match what he was wearing."

"What color was the suit?" Adam asked.

"It was an odd color. Almost taupe and a mauve tweed." She wasn't exactly into fashion like her grandmother, but she knew what matched and what didn't.

"I'm sorry, but I'm not familiar with taupe or mauve."

"Never mind," Sarah said. "Trust me. It clashed."

Adam put his palms up in front of his chest in defense. "Okay. I trust you."

"Oh." Sarah straightened herself in her seat. "He was wearing a flat cap."

Adam was writing on a piece of paper. "And what color was the cap?"

"Gray tweed, I think. It kind of matched his outfit."

Adam continued writing, his pen scratching feverishly. "And when did you see him have the handkerchief?"

"Hey! I'm not one of your witnesses. So, don't treat me like one."

Adam stopped writing and looked up. He placed the pen down. "Of course not," he said, folding his hands.

Sarah sighed. "Look, I saw the man with the red handkerchief inside his breast pocket that day, and then I saw him again, when Rufus and his family came into the boutique the day of his murder. It was after they'd left when I saw the man with the red handkerchief talking to another man I didn't know, but he seemed to know him. But I'm telling you, I never saw him before, and he definitely doesn't dress like he's from around here."

"Okay," Adam said, getting up and grabbing a few things, like his wallet with his badge and his holster. "I think it's time we pay a visit to the Hattingsfords. See if they know who this mystery man is."

Sarah nodded and picked up the evidence bag to hand it back to Adam, when she saw something. She flipped the bag upside down by holding it with her forefinger and thumb at one corner, then took a closer look.

"It looks like there's something stitched on the handkerchief," Sarah said, still eyeing the silk napkin inside the bag. "Looks like a monogram."

Adam scrunched up his forehead. "Let me see," he said with his hand out.

Sarah gave him the bag and he turned it over, looking at it. "O.P." He looked at Sarah. "What do you think it stands for?"

"If it's initials, I don't think the handkerchief belongs to anyone in the Hattingsford family."

Adam nodded. "True, but I think it's time to pay them a visit anyway. I have a lot of unanswered questions and a lot of suspicion around that family."

"Could have been someone outside the family."

"True, but not typically when there's a fortune involved—he was a world-famous magician, after all." Adam walked toward the door with the evidence in his hand and waved her along. "Let's go."

Sarah and Adam stopped at the walkway of the Hattingsfords' residence. Sarah hadn't had a chance to really admire the beautiful, three-story vacation beach house. It was white with baby-blue shutters that captured the lightest blues of the ocean, and it had a front balcony that wrapped around almost the entire house.

"What a lovely place," Sarah said. It reminded her of the Jacobs house, which was a well-known wealthy family in the area. They had passed it and a few other beautiful vacation homes on their way here.

"Yeah," Adam said, looking up. "Now, listen." His tone was deeper this time. More serious. "Let me do the talking. I want to do the unveiling one piece at a time, to gauge their behavior, reactions, and answers. So, don't say anything about the monogram on the handkerchief."

Sarah nodded. She knew withholding information was a tactic used many times to catch someone in a lie. Other times, police purposely didn't release information to see if anyone slipped up by giving up information they thought was public, giving themselves away since they knew more than they should have.

They strolled up the walkway and pressed the doorbell. A small chime could be heard on the stoop from inside. A moment later, a well-dressed Judy opened the door. She looked fresh and was done up, wearing a beautiful floral dress. Her lit-up face turned dim when she saw the officer on her stoop.

"Oh, hello, sir," she said. "I wasn't expecting anyone. Did you find new information regarding my husband?"

"Mrs. Hattingsford," Adam said, "we were wondering if we could speak with you?"

Judy exchanged glances with both of them. "Uh..." Before she could utter another word, her sister was at the door too.

"Who's there?" Faith asked, opening the door wider. "What's going on?"

Adam regarded Faith. "Ma'am, we were wondering if we could ask you and your sister a few questions."

Faith straightened herself. "I don't see what for. We already answered all your questions yesterday. I don't think we know much else. You people deem it a murder, but I still don't see evidence of that. I think he simply fell."

"All our evidence points to a murder."

"What evidence?"

"We have the murder weapon, Ms. Hartlob."

"It's a rock, sir. Not a murder weapon." Faith's head bobbed with conviction, and a few curls escaped her loose bun.

"Faith," Judy said.

Faith continued, ignoring her sister, "He could have fallen, hit his head on the rock, and it went tumbling down the terrain."

Adam sighed. "Why are you dead set on delaying our investigation?"

"My sister is going through enough already. This circus you all are performing is delaying his funeral and other engagements she needs to get through before she can start healing."

Before Adam could respond, a blue sedan pulled up

into the driveway, and Judy's mouth made the shape of an O. "Davey's here!"

She hurried down the walkway toward the car as a tall man with blue eyes got out. Smiling at her, he put his arms out, and they embraced.

Sarah and Adam looked at each other. Then Sarah asked Faith, who had her arms crossed in front of her, "Who's Davey?"

"He's Rufus's youngest brother."

"Oh," Sarah said, turning back to Adam.

"He's already in the case file," Adam told Sarah.

"And he has nothing to do with Rufus's death," Faith said. "None of us do. Before you police start getting all suspicious, remember, his brother just died. Like I said, the sooner you guys stop this nonsense, the sooner my sister and our family can have closure."

Adam shook his head. "I'm not accusing or suspecting Davey of anything. It's just routine to gather background on the family."

Faith narrowed her eyes at Adam. "Good, because he wasn't even in town."

A moment later, Davey and Judy approached them, taking the stony path from the driveway to the walkway that led to the front stoop.

Judy motioned toward Adam and Sarah. "This is

Detective Dunkin and Sarah Shores. She owns a pet boutique place on the boardwalk."

"Actually, it's my grandfather's store. I just help out." Sarah shook the man's hand.

"I'm so glad you are all here trying to get to the bottom of my brother's death. I just came in this afternoon to be here for Judy and Buster and to help with the arrangements. It's just devastating."

"Yes," Sarah said. "It's very devastating, and I'm so sorry for your loss."

Davey's eyes shifted to the ground and then back up to Sarah. "Thank you, ma'am."

There was an awkward silence that lingered for several seconds before Judy cut in. "Why don't we all go inside," she said. "I'll make tea."

The edges of Sarah's mouth ticked up slightly. "That sounds nice."

They all gathered inside. Judy offered for them to take a seat at the dining room table while she scurried into the kitchen to gather the tea.

Sarah couldn't help but look around the vacation home. It was simply stunning. They had an open kitchen with a bar and an island, and off of that was the dining room and living area. A large rug had been placed under the enormous dining room table and chairs. Sarah loved the modern beach decor and the big windows that allowed the natural light to shine through into each room. There were pictures hanging on the wall of Rufus and Judy and their dog, Houdini. Then it dawned on Sarah.

"Where's Houdini?" Sarah asked, now noticing a silver dish in the open kitchen that had a paw print on the front and the Jack Russell's name, Houdini, engraved on the front. Also, there were several toys scattered on the cream-colored carpet in the living area.

"He's out for a walk with Buster," Judy said.

"Probably eating things he shouldn't be," Faith added, waving her finger. "Like those hotdogs at that stand on the boardwalk. I keep telling Buster to stop feeding those dogs to Houdini."

"I'm sure he knows how to make them disappear," Adam said with a chuckle, though no one laughed.

Davey clapped Adam's shoulder and gave him an awkward smile. "Good one, sir."

Sarah couldn't believe Adam would attempt a joke in such a somber situation, but no one seemed to give it much thought as they all took their seats around a large round table in the dining area, by the sliding doors that led to the deck. Even at the table, she could see the Beachside Beacon and the rocks, as well as the ocean water. It was a lovely sight, and Sarah could only imagine the gorgeous sunsets and the rhythmic sound of waves crashing.

"So, Buster has been taking Houdini for walks," Adam said. "Is this something he's always done, or...?"

"He's been going out a lot since Rufus's death," Faith said. "He's taking it pretty hard."

"I see," Adam said.

"Well, I hope you didn't come here to harass Buster."

Sarah swallowed hard, making sure to keep her thoughts about Buster to herself. She still had her suspicions about him. Hankie or no hankie. Buster had good motive, opportunity, and no alibi. Which meant he had all the elements of a murderer, as far as she was concerned.

"So, what is it you wanted to ask us?" Judy set down teacups and took a seat with the rest of them, smoothing her dress beneath her as to not wrinkle it.

Adam cleared his throat. "One of our officers found something at the crime scene that we need to show you. See if you know anything about it."

Sarah pulled out the red handkerchief from her purse and set it on the table. It was still in the evidence bag, to keep it from being compromised. She tried to catch everyone's reaction to the hankie to see if any of them seemed to know something or lie, but they looked more confused than anything else, or indifferent.

"What is that?" Faith asked. "A handkerchief?"

Adam nodded. "Did Rufus own one?"

"No," Judy said, shaking her head. "He never had one of this color."

"How is this considered evidence?" Faith asked, pointing at the bag.

Adam leaned forward toward Faith. "It was found in Rufus's hand."

"It's surely not his," Judy said, her voice an octave higher.

Davey put a hand on Judy's shoulder to keep her calm. "Do you think it could be the perpetrator's?"

Adam shrugged. "It could be."

"A handkerchief?" Faith said. "Now I've heard it all."

"There's something else I want to show you that might help us tremendously in finding Rufus's killer, if this is, indeed, his handkerchief." Adam flipped the bag over and pointed.

Everyone at the table leaned in.

"Looks like a monogram—O.P.," Davey said.

"Yes," Adam said. "Do any of you know someone with those initials?"

Everyone looked at each other, thinking, before shaking their heads.

"Wait," Judy said. Then her face scrunched up. "Oh, no." She shook her head.

"What is it?" Davey asked. "It's okay."

Judy looked at Adam and Sarah. "I think I know what O.P. stands for." She seemed like she was about to faint, and Davey put a hand on her back. "I think I know whose handkerchief this is."

CHAPTER 12

"You know who this handkerchief belongs to?" Adam asked Judy.

Swiping her blonde bangs to either side of her forehead, Judy nodded, not making eye contact. She put a finger up to signify to give her a minute. Getting up, she ignored Davey's comforting hand on her back and left the room. Everyone looked at each other warily, wondering if Judy was all right, but no one spoke. At least, not yet. Then Faith stood. "Maybe I should check on her."

Davey shook his head, pushing his chair back as he stood. "No. It's okay, Faith. You have been doing so much for her. Let me."

Faith put her hands out, as if she was about to reject his offer, when Judy reappeared with a box in her hand.

She carried it to the table for everyone to see and sat down, opening the top. Rummaging, she pulled a folded piece of paper out of an open envelope, handing it to Adam.

Adam sat there with it in his hand for a moment, exchanging glances with Judy, then Sarah. Then he unfolded the piece of paper and began to read. After a few seconds of silence that felt like an eternity, Adam's eyes went wide.

He looked up at Judy. "Do you mind if my colleague reads this?"

Judy shook her head.

Adam handed the letter to Sarah. She felt uneasy reading it in front of so many people, even if she was only going to be reading it to herself. It was still weird to have so many eager eyes on her as she did so.

She opened the letter.

Dear Rufus,

I have been trying to reach you for some time now. I saw your grand performance in New York. Remember, I know your secrets. Write me back. I'll be waiting. If not, I will find you.

Orlando Prince

Realizing her mouth was hanging open just like Adam's had after he was done reading the note, Sarah locked eyes with Adam.

"Well," Faith said. "What does it say?" She glanced back and forth between Adam and Sarah, but neither spoke. "What's going on?" She snatched the letter from Sarah and read it over.

Faith's hand covered her mouth as she looked up from the letter. "What secrets? You think this Orlando Prince did it?" She pointed to the handwritten note in her hand.

"We don't know," Adam said. "That's what we are trying to find out."

Sarah regarded Judy. "Is there a return address on the envelope?"

Judy nodded and handed Adam the envelope. He took a look at it and let out a short chuckle. Then he handed it to Sarah.

"Orlando, Florida," Sarah read out loud and shook her head. Orlando wasn't incredibly far from Cascade Cove. If Sarah had to guess, it was a three-hour drive, but that was only if you made a straight shot on I-95. "Should have known. The man's name is Orlando."

"I have several letters I kept from this guy," Judy said. "I told Rufus that he should call the police. At least have them put it on file, just in case. I should have done it myself." Judy's shoulders bobbed when she put her head in her hands.

Concern instantly washed over Faith's face as she moved in to comfort her sister.

Judy looked up, her face scrunched up in distress. "Do you think he killed my husband?"

"I don't know, Mrs. Hattingsford," Adam said.

Faith, who was stroking her sister's hair, lifted her head. "Well, you know where he lives. Find him and question him," she demanded.

Sarah exchanged glances with Adam. Now, Faith seemed to be on board with the idea that this possibly crazed-obsessed fan could be the murderer.

"If you don't mind, I'd like to take this letter as evidence," Adam said. "You said there were more, Mrs. Hattingsford?"

Judy, head still buried in her hands, nodded without looking up.

"Take the whole box," Faith said. "Just find this guy."

Davey, who seemed stunned by all the commotion, got to his feet. "I think that's enough for one day. Allow me to walk you both to the door."

Sarah and Adam stood in unison. Adam scooped up the box while walking around the two sisters.

As he turned toward the door, Faith's head popped up from hugging her sister. "You find the person who did this and you do it quickly. I'm not sure how much more my sister can take of this." Her eyes were like stone, boring through Adam.

Adam nodded and waved Sarah on to follow him to the door, where Davey was waiting.

"I'm sorry we had to meet under these circumstances, sir," Davey said. "I think the evidence stacks up pretty high against this Orlando guy. I hope you find him quickly."

"We'll do our best, Mr. Hattingsford."

Davey shook his head. "'Mr. Hattingsford' is too formal. Just call me Davey."

Adam gave him a curt nod and said, "I'll let you and your family know if there's any new information."

"I appreciate that, sir," Davey said as he opened the door. "It was lovely to meet you, Ms. Sarah."

Sarah smiled. "Likewise," she said before stepping out onto the stoop, followed by Adam. As soon as they were out of the house, Davey closed the door.

Sarah looked at Adam. "That was rough."

"Yeah," Adam said. Then he held up the box of letters. "I guess we know what our next job is."

"Thank you for your time, ma'am." Adam hung up the

phone. He looked at Sarah, who was sitting on the other side of the table at the police station. They were in a white room with only a table and three chairs. Letters and papers were strewn across the large rectangular table, which was cold to the touch, probably because of the air conditioning being on full blast, despite the fact that the sweltering summer days were over. Granted, it was still warm enough to sport a tank and shorts and take a dip in the pool, but it was a far cry from the heat stroke she'd felt several months ago. Maybe they were in the interrogation room, and this was how they tortured their suspects into confessing their crimes.

Sarah tried to avoid the shock of the icy desk altogether by reading the letters with her arms hovering slightly above the desk or by leaning back in her chair.

"Any luck?" Sarah asked.

"Nope. I called Orlando Prince's residence, and there was no answer. I just got off with a secretary at his work, and she says he's on vacation."

"I knew it," Sarah said. "I bet you that he's the mysterious guy I've been seeing with the flat cap and odd suit roaming around Cascade Cove ever since Rufus and his family arrived. Everywhere I saw Rufus, that guy seemed to be lurking around."

Adam let out a heavy breath. "You could be right. We just have to find the guy, but if he is the murderer, he has probably fled already. I mean, have you seen him since Rufus's unfortunate demise?"

Sarah shook her head. "Wish I could say I have, but I haven't."

"How are the letters going?"

"There are a lot in here. Mostly from regular fans asking for autographs and such. I found another from Orlando Prince that says he tried his house."

"What?"

"Yeah, it's right here." Sarah handed him the letter.

Adam read it over. "Oh my. This is definitely a stalker. No question."

"His obsession certainly sounds deadly. He not only follows Rufus but tells him he will track him down. And in this letter, he states that he showed up at his house, and when no one answered, he was sad and disappointed. It's kind of creepy."

Adam rubbed his chin anxiously. "We need to find this guy." He looked at the stacks of letters spilling out of the box. "Give me some of those. I'll help you."

Sarah pushed a bunch of unread letters toward Adam, and they continued scanning each one, looking for more clues. Soon, it was late, and they decided to call it a night. Sarah couldn't believe she had spent the entire day working on the case, and the better part of the evening into the night reading letters. She pulled out her cell phone and saw she had several missed messages. Two from her cousin and one from Grandpa.

The two from Emma were just messages about her sweaters she was selling, and the message from her grandfather was him asking if she would be home for dinner. She felt guilty missing their messages, but she knew they would understand, especially after hearing about everything that had happened that day. Then her phone buzzed again.

This time it was a message from Teek:

Hey dudette! Meet up at the sand dune hideout for Surfing Santas at 7 tomorrow.

The message was also followed by a winking-face emoji, then a Santa, a surfboard, and a wave. Sarah groaned.

"What?" Adam asked.

"I forgot about the Surfing Santas event tomorrow!"

"Oh," Adam said. He sounded a little disappointed, which surprised Sarah, since lately Adam had been asking her to butt out of his investigations. "Go. Enjoy yourself."

"But what about—"

"It's your first Surfing Santa."

"What about you?"

"Me? I've seen it too many times. It's really a nonevent for me."

Sarah gave her *are you sure* look.

"It's okay. Go." Then Adam looked down at his feet. "Besides, you don't want to miss Teek. It's his favorite, and he works hard to entertain every year."

"That's very big of you to say."

"Hey, what can I say," Adam said, blushing slightly, "I'm a big guy."

Sarah snorted in laughter, then quickly covered her mouth. "I'm sorry. I didn't mean to laugh at you."

"That's okay." Adam shrugged. "Kind of tempted to see your reaction to a bunch of crazies surfing in red suits and long beards."

Sarah laughed again, walking toward the door.

"I'm still waiting to see a flamingo in a Santa hat," Sarah added as she walked out.

Before she closed the door, she could hear Adam say, "Trust me. You will!"

CHAPTER 13

Sarah woke up to her alarm in the dark room that she shared with Emma. Groggily, she rolled over and reached for her cell phone, which was sitting on her nightstand. The screen of her cell phone was illuminated, and the time was blinking in rhythm with the tune she had programmed to wake her. She shut off the alarm and turned on the light so she could see. The first thing she noticed—other than Winston's rhythmic snoring—was a pair of red-and-white striped tights and a red sweatshirt lying on her desk with a note.

A tinge of guilt filled Sarah as she remembered that she'd gotten in late last night after everyone had gone to bed. She hadn't noticed the clothes that were prepared for her because she'd decided to use her cell phone light to navigate the room so she wouldn't wake her cousin.

Sarah pulled off the covers and walked over to the small pile of clothes, neatly folded on the desk. She opened the note:

Sarah,

Sorry we missed each other last night…

Sarah didn't know what Emma was sorry about. It was Sarah who hadn't come home till late last night. She continued reading,

I ordered this outfit for you to wear for your first Surfing Santa adventure. I hope you like it. Put it on, and I'll see you in the kitchen!

Love,
Emma

P.S. Don't forget the flip flops!

Sarah looked down and saw there was a pair of white flip flops on the floor in front of her desk. She turned to Winston, who was yawning and slowly pulling himself up.

"I guess I better get ready," Sarah said to Winston.

He responded with another yawn and a grunt.

Sarah scuffled into the bathroom to wash up and returned to the prepared clothes. She opened the sweatshirt to gauge its size and noticed that it had a Santa balancing on a surfboard, wearing sunglasses and shorts with little palm trees on them. It read, "I wiped out with the Surfing Santas" across the top, and on the bottom, it read, "at Cascade Cove Beaches."

Sarah smiled before slipping it over her head. It fit perfectly and was cozy. Winston plopped back down in his bed. Apparently, it was too early for the corgi.

When she walked out to the kitchen, she saw Rugby was already devouring his breakfast. Her cousin was pouring two mugs of coffee at the counter, and was wearing the same exact sweater and tights, except her sweatshirt was white and she had on red flip flops, alternating the red and white colors that Sarah had on. Sarah shook her head.

"We look like a couple of candy canes," Sarah said, tugging on the bottom of her sweatshirt.

"Perfect," Emma said with a wink. She handed Sarah a mug of coffee with the cream and sugar already added, just the way she liked it. "It's your first Surfing Santas experience and you have to look the part."

"Does 'looking the part' require a nutty and absurd dress code?"

"Yes," Emma said, taking a sip of her coffee. "And trust me, if you don't look completely nutty and absurd, you won't fit in. Think Wacky Wednesday during high school spirit week, only this time, it's Christmas themed."

Sarah gave her a confused look.

"You don't have that in New York, Sarah?"

"We have spirit week, but I don't know what a Wacky Wednesday is."

Emma shook her head. "You poor souls." She set her coffee down on the counter. "Just think, the tackier and the more mismatched, the better."

Sarah chuckled, giving her cousin the okay sign. "Got it." Then she looked around. "So, where's Grandpa? He lives for this sort of thing."

Just then, Larry popped around the corner, sporting a green Hawaiian button-down with images of little islands with palm trees and Santas lounging on the beach drinking cocktails. He also had on candy cane-striped suspenders, hooked to a pair of red Bermuda shorts, and flip flops. But the most outlandish part of his costume was the white beard and the red Christmas hat he wore on top of his straw hat. It was everything Sarah would expect from her Grandpa and more.

"Grandpa!" Sarah said. "You look...merry."

"Darn!" Larry said, snapping his fingers. "I was going for jolly and hip."

Sarah chuckled. "You know you're wearing two hats?"

"Oh." Larry pulled down his sunglasses and looked up under the brim of his straw hat. He pointed at it, returning his gaze to Sarah. "I need this hat to keep the sun out of my eyes, and I need the Santa hat for the event. You've got to be festive, you know, or you won't fit in."

"I heard," Sarah said.

"Speaking of the Santa hat, check this out." Larry reached inside his Santa hat and clicked it on. The hat lit up, playing "We Wish You a Merry Christmas." The lights in the white edges of the hat and the ball at the end twinkled in rhythm to the music. Rugby looked up from his bowl and barked at the musical hat. Then he sat down, putting up a paw, and whined.

Sarah and Emma both chuckled.

"All right," Larry said, turning the hat off. "I get it, Rugby. You're not a fan."

Then Sarah looked at the time. "We better get a move on. Teek said he wants us to meet him at the Sand Dune Hideout at seven."

"Well, then," Larry said. "We better get some breakfast and head down to the beach."

An hour later, Sarah, Emma, and Larry were flip-flopping down toward the beach. The sun hadn't risen yet, but she could see the glow in the horizon toward the water. Behind her, she could still see the crescent moon hanging in the purple twilit sky.

Along the way, Larry had gotten caught up in a conversation with Henry Fudderman from Fudderman's Bakery. He was dressed up for the festivities too, sporting a full-fledged old-fashioned Santa suit—which suited him well, since he looked a lot like Jolly ol' Saint Nick with his protruding, round belly and his rosy cheeks. He even had on the wire-rimmed glasses and coat.

Because Sarah was worried about being late meeting Teek, Emma and Sarah continued on toward the beach without Grandpa.

"So, what happened yesterday?" Emma asked.

Sarah recapped her visit with Teek and told Emma about what he'd said about Buster leaving the bar at least twenty minutes before midnight.

"That would give Buster more than enough time to get back to the house and commit the act," Emma said.

"Yes. That's what I said to Adam. But then he pulled out a red handkerchief from his drawer. Says that it was found clutched inside the magician's hand, and it has the initials O.P. stitched into it."

"Wow. Do they know who it belongs to?"

"That's the thing," Sarah said. "Remember the man I'd seen outside the store after Rufus and his family left?"

Emma nodded.

"I saw that handkerchief in his front breast pocket," Sarah said.

"Are you sure?"

"I can't say one hundred percent, but it stuck out to me because it didn't match his outfit. It was a strange addition to his suit. Anyway, I saw the man several times before Rufus's unfortunate demise. But since then, he's disappeared."

"You're right. Now that's suspicious. Though, I wonder if Buster and this strange man could've been working together."

"I hadn't thought of that. But see, we went to the Hattingsfords' and spoke with Judy. She said she thinks she knows what O.P. stands for."

Emma's eyes grew wide. "No way!"

"Yup. She had a box of fan mail and gave us a letter by a crazed fan that seemed to be stalking Rufus, and the letter was signed by a man named Orlando Prince."

"Never heard of him," Emma said. "So, we have Buster, who has motive since he had just found out that

Rufus was behind the mishap during his big show that cost him his career, as well as opportunity since he lied about his alibi. And we have a mysterious man who could be the owner of the red handkerchief and now has disappeared since the murder."

"Precisely," Sarah said.

"Or it could have been his wife and sister-in-law. They would benefit from his fortune, and even more so if he were dead. They also had the means and opportunity."

Sarah nodded. "Or anyone else Rufus has angered with his sour attitude and bitterness."

"Right. Like that mother and her son who asked Rufus to perform a trick for him."

The early morning breeze picked up, and Sarah swiped a flyaway hair from her face. She could feel that they were getting closer to the water. "But I think we are on to something with the handkerchief. You have to admit, it's incredible evidence. Especially if it was clutched in the hand of the victim."

"Didn't you say that there wasn't a struggle? That it seemed the perpetrator bumped him over the head with a rock by sneaking up behind him?"

Sarah thought a moment. Emma was right. There were no defensive wounds on Rufus, and therefore, they could only assume at this point that he had been unaware of his attacker. Or maybe that he had even known his killer. Could Rufus have known Orlando Prince?

They had just about reached the beach, making their way down the ramp to the sand. Sarah couldn't help but gawk at the beautiful sunrise over the water. She'd seen many sunsets in her life, including the ones she'd watched from the Ferris wheel, but those didn't compare to the sun rising above the ocean line. Colors were strewn across the sky, reflecting off the water like glistening fireflies of every hue, dancing.

"Sarah!"

A voice interrupted her thoughts.

Emma pointed. "There he is."

Teek was at the Sand Dune Hideout, holding his board upright and waving. She could tell he'd been prepping it. They made their way over to him. Just as expected, he was wearing the whole getup. The Santa costume with the shorts, flip flops, sunglasses, and white beard. He'd even tucked his long, sandy locks under his Santa hat, and added some white sunscreen to the tip of his nose. It was a nice touch.

"Hey, dudettes!" he called to them as they approached. He chuckled as they stopped in front of him. "Diggin' the sweats."

Sarah couldn't help but think it was odd to hear Santa with a surfer accent and using lingo.

"Diggin' your costume too," Sarah said.

"Ha! This Santa's Christmas wish is to chase a big swell." Teek put up his fists and yelled, "Yeah!"

Emma furrowed her eyebrows. "What?"

"You know," Teek said. "Boogie down the barrel. Get tubed." He used his right hand to imitate him surfing down a straight line. Then he chuckled again.

Sarah turned to her cousin. "He's saying he hopes to hit a good wave and surf down through the barrel of it."

"Yeah," Teek said. "She gets it."

Emma just shook her head.

Before Sarah knew it, the beach was peppered with little red-suited Santas as far as the eye could see, most of them carrying surfboards under their arms. A few were trying to catch some short waves before the event started.

Then Sarah heard her name being called. She looked around and saw that one of the Santas was waving at her. Sarah squinted. Who could it be? He started running toward her, and as he came closer, he began to look familiar.

"Adam?" she called out to the man in the distance. "What are you doing here?"

CHAPTER 14

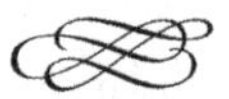

"I'm so glad I found you," Adam said, trying to catch his breath. He was also dressed as Santa in shorts and had the beard like most of the other Santas who hadn't grown out their own gray whiskers, but his was pulled down around his neck.

"Well, well," Sarah said. "Look at you." She laughed. "I see you decided to not only join us, but also come as Santa!"

"Ha-ha," Adam said. "Laugh it up. Sheriff Wheeler thought it would be a good idea for me to take a break from the Hattingsford case and come down here sort of undercover. Watch over the event."

"I see," Sarah said. "Sounds like fun."

"Well, at least I found you."

Teek strolled up to them, kicking sand with every step. "Dude!" he cried. "Here to catch some waves, too?"

"Oh, I don't—" Adam started.

"Remember what I taught you, chicken wing?" Teek asked.

Sarah lifted her eyebrows, "Did he just call you 'chicken wing'?"

Adam put up a hand. "Don't ask."

"C'mon, broski! Let's hit some waves together."

"Now, what is he calling you?" Emma asked.

"Bro," Adam said.

Emma still looked bewildered.

Adam sighed. "Like, we're such close friends that we might as well be brothers."

"Oh," she said, almost silently.

"Listen, Teek," Adam said. "I didn't bring my board, and I'm here to monitor the event."

"Ah, on the job. Undercover and such," Teek said.

"Yeah," Adam said quietly.

"That's cool, dude." Teek ripped off his Santa coat, and a small crowd formed around them. It was then that Sarah realized that he wasn't wearing a shirt underneath, revealing his tanned abs and a red necktie that must've been hidden under his coat. He threw his Santa coat down, and the small crowd that had gathered cheered, hooting and hollering.

"See ya later, newbs!" Teek said as he took off toward the water with his board. The three of them watched as the crowd followed him, waving their arms and screaming.

"Must he always take off his shirt?" Adam asked.

"You're lucky that's all he takes off," Emma said. "His mom once told me that when he was a toddler, he'd strip daily and take off buck naked out of the house to the water."

Sarah laughed. "One day, I have to meet her."

"You should," Emma said. "She's a hoot."

Sarah, Emma, and Adam watched Teek as he took on several waves. He was showing off his many perfected stunts in the water. As some of the surfing Santas were able to ride the simple waves and stay balanced on their boards, many others wiped out and ran the boards into each other.

After a while of watching hundreds of red suits bob and glide in the water, they walked around a bit. The beach was crowded with people dressed up as various Christmas characters like elves and gingerbread men. Many of the young women were dressed in red or green tutus with tights and a lei around their necks. There was even a man completely decked out as Yukon Cornelius from *Rudolph the Red-Nosed Reindeer,* including the earmuffs, the red beard, mittens, and axe.

Sarah couldn't believe the amount of effort many had put into their costumes, yet the crowd of smiling faces gave her a sense of warmth and community. It was times like this that Sarah knew she had made the right choice in leaving New York City to be with family and friends.

"Hey, Sarah, look!" Emma said, pointing to the stage that was set up at the back of the beach, closer to the boardwalk. There was a man with white hair on stage, who wore a bright-red Hawaiian shirt, sunglasses, and sandals, playing Mele Kalikimaka on a ukulele. There was an elderly man that was dressed a lot like the man on stage, bouncing to the music and singing along. That's when Sarah realized what her cousin was pointing at.

"Grandpa!" Emma yelled, now pulling Sarah by the hand. Sarah turned to Adam, quickly grabbing his hand so she didn't lose him. As they pulled each other through the crowd to Grandpa, the man on staged acknowledged Larry in the small audience.

"Hey, sir! Come up and help me sing!" The man pulled Larry onto the stage just as they reached him, and they sang the rest of the song while Sarah, Emma, and Adam danced along to the music.

Then the music picked up with various drums as a group of hula dancers took over the stage. They started swaying their hips around Larry, whose cheeks flushed.

"Dance, Grandpa!" Sarah yelled, cupping her hands around her mouth.

"Yeah, Grandpa!" Emma shouted. "Move those hips!"

They all laughed as Larry tried to keep up with the hula dancers. They surrounded him, smiling. But when it became too hard for Larry to keep up, he resorted to circling his arms in front of his chest and doing his own little jig.

When it was over, there was a roaring applause from the audience as the hula dancers each blew Larry a kiss. He placed both of his hands on his chest as if he were in love and blew them all a kiss back. Then, the man who was playing the ukulele grabbed Larry by the shoulder and whispered something in his ear. He handed him what looked like a slip of paper, and Larry put the piece of paper in his pocket. He then waved at the man as he headed off the stage. The man gave him a smile, joining the applause.

"Grandpa," Sarah said. "That was amazing!"

"I know," Larry said. "So much fun!"

"What did the guy say to you?" Emma asked.

"And what did he give you?" Sarah added.

Grandpa Larry reached into his front breast pocket and pulled out a white card. It said, "Murph's Ukes."

Emma raised an eyebrow.

"He owns a ukulele shop about fifteen minutes away," Larry said. "I think I've passed it before. He says I should stop by and buy a ukulele."

"So, he was trying to sell to you," Emma said.

Larry thrust out his chin. "He also said I had a nice singing voice, and maybe we can get together so he can teach me the uke and we can perform together."

Emma crossed her arms in front of her chest. "Grandpa, don't you think you have enough hobbies?"

Larry cocked his head as if he didn't understand what his granddaughter was trying to say.

Emma waved her words away with a chuckle. "Never mind."

"Is Teek in the water yet?" Larry asked.

Adam gestured to the surfing Santa in the midst of doing a handstand on his surfboard. A small crowd that had gathered to watch were chanting and cheering. "I'm surprise you hadn't noticed."

"Ah," Larry said. "He has a way with the girls."

Just then, Sarah heard feedback from one of the speakers, and she directed her attention to the stage. A middle-aged man in a green-and-red plaid suit and a necktie to match was at the microphone.

"Oh, it's the mayor," Adam said. "He speaks at the event every year."

The tanned man with silver hair and mustache began to speak. "Welcome, people of Cascade Cove and our guests. Thank you for coming and being a part of our tradition—the fifth annual Surfing Santas!" His voice boomed louder on the last part and the crowd erupted in cheers and applause.

"I can't thank you all enough," the mayor continued. "Each and every one of you make this day a little more special. When Teek Turlant started this event five years ago, he was a lone Santa catching the waves."

"You mean gettin' tubed, Mayor, sir!" Teek shouted from the back.

The mayor chuckled and pointed to Teek. "Yes, of course!" All of a sudden, the mayor's accent turned to that of a surfer. "Gettin' tubed! And going down the wave, taking a bottom turn, going up to the top, and doin' a high-line wrap!"

"Yeah!" Teek yelled.

The crowd remained silent except for the few surfer guys and gals who understood the lingo. Though, this one even got Sarah a little confused.

Teek let out another "yeah," and then shouted, "This dude gets it!"

Sarah turned around to see Teek pointing at the mayor on stage. Though, someone else caught her eye.

Was it…It couldn't be. Sarah squinted, shielding her

eyes from the sun. The man had his face turned to his left.

The mayor continued his speech. "I just want to wish everyone a…"

Sarah waited for the man to face forward again so she could get a better look.

Adam nudged her. "What's up? What are you looking at?"

It was then that Sarah realized she was being extremely obvious. Being closest to the stage, she was turned in the opposite direction of everyone else in the crowd. But she didn't care. She had to know. She zeroed in on the man, who was unaware of her undivided attention.

Adam turned to see what she was looking at.

The mayor was still speaking in the background. "… in this joyous time. We come together…"

When Adam couldn't figure it out, he asked her again.

"The man…by Teek…" Sarah started.

Adam looked again. "What man?"

"The one wearing the flat cap and the tweed suit. The mystery man."

Sarah could tell Adam had finally caught sight of the person Sarah was looking at.

The mayor's voice was still booming, "…a very

special Cascade Cove Christmas!"

The crowd cheered once more, and the man in the flat cap faced forward. It *was* him!

"Sarah," Adam said anxiously.

"It's him, Adam," she said. "That's the mystery man. Rufus's stalker."

CHAPTER 15

The mayor finished his speech and the crowd erupted one final time before dispersing. Sarah followed Adam closely as he weaved through the crowd heading back to the water to surf. The man had also begun walking away, and for a moment, they lost him.

Sarah scanned the crowd, her eyes darting from one unrecognizable face to the next, searching for the mystery man or his flat cap, but the fellow that wore it wasn't very tall. She whipped her head around in pure desperation—would she ever find the man?

She shifted her gaze, and was surprised to spot the man heading down the beach.

"There he is!" Sarah shouted to Adam, but apparently her voice was loud enough for the man with the tweed suit to hear her, too. He turned around and looked at Sarah.

"Hey!" Adam shouted. "Hey, you!"

The man locked eyes with Adam, and he immediately turned whiter than the Christmas ghost that came to visit Mr. Scrooge. The man began to run.

"Hey! Get back here!" Adam yelled, as he took off into a sprint. "Police!"

Sarah was hot on Adam's heels. Behind her, someone else hollered, "Get him!" but she didn't turn around to see who it was, afraid she'd lose sight of the man.

Before she knew it, they were in a mad dash to chase down the mystery man in the tweed suit. Adam ended up gaining distance between them. Sarah hadn't realized how difficult it was to run in the sand. Her legs would quickly grow tired if she didn't figure something out. She wasn't about to lose this guy again.

Kicking off her flip flops, she tried to stay light on her feet as to not sink too far into the dry sand, but it only made her situation worse. She decided to make her way to the wet sand by the water, so she could gain solid footing.

That was when she heard wet feet slapping behind her. Was someone chasing her? She looked back and realized that she was followed by not only her cousin but several Santas, two elves, the Grinch, a gingerbread man, and a partridge in a pear tree. No, really. There was a person dressed as a Christmas tree trailing behind them all.

Up ahead, Adam was shouting, "Wait! Stop!" But Sarah knew that Adam catching up to the guy was still a long shot. And the Grinch, with his evil grin, was gaining on her! She wasn't sure what side this green creature was on, but she wasn't about to slow down to find out. So, she picked up her pace.

Out of nowhere, a man surfing on the water, wearing a red suit, passed her. She turned to get a better look—it was a surfing Santa cutting up ahead of everyone, including the mystery man. As the wave rolled in, the surfing Santa glided onto shore, hopped off his board, and started running. Within a couple of short seconds, he intercepted the mystery man before he could react, bulldozing him into the sandy ground.

Sarah almost fell flat on her face herself after witnessing the capture, but she regained her footing and slowed down to a more appropriate speed before approaching the scene. The people who had taken part in the chase also slowed down and cheered as Santa ripped off his hat, revealing his bleached-blond hair tied up in a bun.

His name escaped Sarah's lips. "Teek!"

Adam pounced on the man with the tweed suit,

rolling him onto his stomach and pulling his arms behind his back so that he could apprehend him. The man wiggled under him, still trying to break free.

"Ah, dude! Did you see that?" Teek asked. "I nailed the guy!"

"Thank you, Teek," Adam said, still holding the man down with a knee in his back.

Teek waved his words away, grinning. "No problem, chicken wing."

Adam shook his head. "Will you try to refrain from calling me that when I'm at work?"

Teek inhaled sharply through his perfectly aligned teeth. "Oh. Sorry, broski."

Adam turned his attention to the man under him, with his face in the sand. "Are you Orlando Prince?" Adam asked in his authoritative voice. Two security officers were now present.

The man lifted his head. "Yeah. What's this all about?"

Adam waved at one of the officers to hand him his handcuffs. "You're under arrest for the murder of Rufus Hattingsford."

The crowd gasped, including the mystery man, Orlando Prince, himself.

At the police station, Sarah was sitting in the waiting area along with the Grinch, a couple of Santas, and the gingerbread man. Being completely aware of her surroundings, she felt certain that Orlando Prince, murderer or not, had to feel rather weird being questioned by a Santa in Bermuda shorts and flip flops, after being chased down by two candy canes and a Christmas parade.

Emma walked into the police station, and Sarah met her at the reception desk. Emma said, "I took Grandpa home. He can't stop talking about the 'shake down' at the Surfing Santas event. He can't wait to tell Grandma when she gets back from the cruise."

Sarah couldn't wait either. Though, she knew Grandma Ruth was most likely wrapped up in her own wacky adventures on the cruise ship, and that they would swap stories soon. But, unfortunately, that wouldn't be until after the holidays.

Officer Deats gazed up from his desk. "Emma Shores," he said with a twinkle in his dark-brown eyes. "I need you to sign in." He tapped the clipboard.

"You look stunning today," he said as she signed her name on the form.

Emma glared at him warily.

"I mean 'nice,'" Deats said. His gaze lowered to her tights. "I like the...uh...pants."

Emma put the pen down and glanced at her red-and-white striped bottoms before regarding Deats. "They're called tights," she said before walking away, leaving Sarah there. Emma stepped over to the plastic chairs and took a seat, motioning Sarah to hurry up.

Sarah leaned over the desk toward Officer Deats. "You know, Deats, she's taken."

Officer Deats shrugged. "You can't blame me for trying. Besides, she's not really 'taken' until Mark seals the deal."

"You're, like, twice her age."

The officer pondered her last statement, then said, "Not quite."

Sarah chuckled, shaking her head in disbelief. "Fat chance, Deats," she said, walking away to join her cousin in the waiting area.

When Sarah took a seat, Emma turned to her. "What's with the gang of Christmas misfits?" Emma asked, gesturing to the people from the beach who helped chase down Orlando Prince.

"Adam asked them to come down to write a statement. He wants as many witnesses as possible in case Orlando is injured in any way. He needs proof the man ran from authorities. And did you forget that we look like a couple of sad candy canes ourselves?"

The woman dressed as a Christmas tree waved at Emma with a smile.

Emma sent back a small wave filled with skepticism before turning back to Sarah. "Where's Adam?"

"They're in the process of booking the guy."

Just then, Adam came out from the door behind Officer Deats's desk. He was now dressed in his uniform, holding a manila folder in his hand. "Sarah." He motioned to her to follow him. "Emma, I'm glad you're here. I'll need a written statement from you, too."

"Hey!" the Grinch said. "We've been waiting here forever! I've got things to do, and I'd like to get out of here before next Christmas!"

"I'll send someone out to get you guys," Adam said.

The Grinch plopped back down in his chair with a harrumph. "This is the last time I try to help the police."

Adam sighed, then gestured to the door. Sarah and Emma followed him. "Sheriff Wheeler is off duty for the day. And Melinda doesn't work weekends."

Sarah had a feeling she knew where Adam was going with this, but knew he wasn't going to ask for her to participate in the questioning forthright.

"Sarah, you pick up on things that others don't," Adam said. "And I just have to get Wheeler on board with the idea of having you help us with these sorts of cases."

"I don't think he'll ever agree to that."

Adam stopped. "He allows a medium to help us with missing persons cases." Adam arched an eyebrow.

"Wow," Emma said. "Is the medium good?"

"Well," Adam said, cocking his head side to side. "She's decent. Hits about fifty-fifty."

Emma glanced at Sarah. "That's pretty good."

"Yeah," Adam said, "but we don't know if it's just good guessing or if she really has mystical powers."

Emma crossed her arms. "A skeptic, I see."

Adam let out a chuckle. "Not always. There are things in this world we can't explain. But anyway..." He shifted his gaze to Sarah. "Maybe if you could just watch from outside?"

Sarah nodded. "Of course, I will. That is, as long as I don't get you into any trouble."

"If Sheriff Wheeler finds out, I may be in some heat, but I won't get fired. He needs me to solve these murders. And I need you."

"Can I watch too?" Emma asked.

Adam put his hands on his hips. "As long as I get that written statement from you. I just called Officer Finley, and I'm going to have him collect all the statements as soon as he gets in."

"Deal," Emma said.

They continued walking down the hall to a room

with a large, dark window. Adam flipped a switch, and the window revealed Orlando Prince sitting in a plastic chair at a large table. It was the same room that she had been in with Adam just yesterday while they rifled through hundreds of Rufus's fan letters. No wonder the room was so cold.

"You need a pen and pad for notes?" Adam asked.

"No," Sarah said. "I do better just listening." To Sarah, it wasn't always about what was said so much as how things were said. Besides, she had learned from being a student in school that when she took notes during a lecture, she'd miss a lot. It was better to just sit back and absorb as much as possible.

Adam gave her a curt nod, then stormed inside the room with purpose.

Sarah and Emma faced the window that Sarah now knew only appeared to be a mirror to those inside the room.

"Orlando Prince," she could hear Adam say to the man.

Orlando locked eyes with Adam as the detective sat across the table from him. Adam plopped the folder onto the table.

"Do you know why you're here?" Adam asked.

Orlando didn't speak. He just shook his head.

"Where were you Wednesday night between 11:30 and midnight?"

There was another moment of silence.

"Well?" Adam asked, slouching in his chair and crossing his arms.

"I don't remember off the top of my head," Orlando said. "I don't even remember what I had to eat for dinner last night. Just give me a minute to think."

"You've had enough time to think up an alibi."

"I didn't kill my friend!"

Adam perked up. "Your friend? You mean, your victim."

"I didn't kill him!"

"I have evidence stacked up to my ears that all points to you." Adam used his hand to show how much.

Orlando shook his head with conviction. "No, you don't, because I didn't do it."

"So, then why'd you run from law enforcement?"

"I didn't know you were the police! I just saw a bunch of Santas, elves, and Christmas cookies chasing me."

Adam huffed. "I said, 'police.'"

Orlando shrugged. "I didn't hear that. All I saw was a mob of people after me."

Adam glared at the man for a long moment before grumbling to himself. Then he opened the big manila envelope and pulled out the handkerchief, which was still wrapped in the evidence bag. "Is this yours?" He pushed the bag and it slid to a halt in front of Orlando.

Orlando put his hand up to his empty breast pocket. "I…I've been looking everywhere for that. Where'd you find it?"

"Clutched in the helpless, dead hand of your 'friend.'"

Orlando's eyes grew wide before his forehead scrunched up in confusion.

Adam pointed to the bag. "You want to explain that?"

"I can't."

Adam slid his hand into the manila envelope and pulled out several letters that were already opened and also held in plastic bags. Sarah knew immediately they were the letters Orlando had written to Rufus.

"And these?" Adam said, rotating the letters with his fingertips so that Orlando could read them.

Orlando glared at them, his eyes darting from line to line. "Yes, I wrote these to Rufus. I was hoping to touch base with him here."

"How long have you been obsessively stalking Rufus?"

"Stalking? I'm not stalking him."

"You say here that you know his secrets. What secrets?"

Orlando stammered, trying to find words.

"And here"—Adam pointed again—"you say that you will find him. And in this one"—Adam shoved the other letter closer to Orlando's chest—"you admit to going to his house, and since he wasn't there, you threaten to track him down."

Orlando furrowed his brows. "I wasn't threatening him."

"So, you have a good explanation for these letters?"

"Yes, I do," Orlando said, crossing his arms.

"And the secret?" Adam asked.

Orlando leaned forward, locking eyes with Adam. "I know the secrets behind his magic tricks because my father taught him. We grew up together. I'm not a murderer, and I wouldn't kill Rufus."

Adam was unmoving, surveying the man's eyes as he spoke.

Orlando continued, "Rufus was my childhood best friend."

CHAPTER 16

Adam remained seated across from Orlando Prince at a large table in the interrogation room.

"Didn't expect that answer," Emma said, exchanging glances with Sarah.

"Me neither," Sarah said.

They returned their attention to what was transpiring on the other side of the two-way mirror.

"You ever hear of Orlando King?" Orlando asked.

"No, I haven't," Adam said.

Orlando sighed. "He was my father—and a popular magician in Orlando, Florida. Everyone knew him there."

"Wait. So, you and your dad both share the same first name but have different last names?"

"No. My father's legal name is Frederic Prince. He only changed his name to Orlando King for his stage name. And then he named me Orlando."

Adam paused, seemingly trying to wrap his head around the names. "So, what does this have to do with Rufus?"

"My father dreamed that I would follow in his footsteps, and so he taught me magic, but I wasn't very good. I'd practice at recess in grade school, and that's when I met Rufus. He knew nothing about magic, but he was enthralled by it. He started coming to my house on a nightly basis, and eventually, so did his brother, Buster. Tricks that would take me weeks, sometimes months to master, Rufus would get in merely hours. At first, it was frustrating, but then I got into baseball, and then in high school, I was into girls. Magic was for children. But that wasn't true for Rufus. He mastered it and continued meeting with my father for more training."

"That must've angered you, you know, your father giving Rufus all the attention."

"No, not really. I was a testy teenager, and Rufus got my dad off my back. Though, I've regretted not appreciating my dad as much since he's passed."

"When did he die?"

Orlando's eyes welled up. "Six months ago." His voice cracked, and he paused before clearing his throat. "I had been trying to get in touch with Rufus because he makes me feel closer to him somehow. I guess it's the magic. It's familiar. He knew all my father's tricks and performed them just like him. But I understand that he's busy and that he has a lot of fans. I assumed that that was why he hadn't answered my letters.

"I could never murder Rufus. I just wanted to reminisce with him. Devour the fond memories he had of my father when I was too distracted to give him the time of day."

Orlando broke down, sobbing in his hands. Adam looked at the window—though Sarah knew he couldn't see where she was exactly, it still felt like he was speaking to her, asking what she thought. She didn't know what to think, though she was starting to question Orlando Prince's involvement in the murder as she watched the flood of tears roll down his face.

Adam and Sarah were in the lounge, getting coffee. Adam had stopped the interrogation for now, allowing Emma to work on her statement.

He took a sip of his coffee and stuck his hand in his pocket. "What do you think, Sarah?"

"About what?" she asked, adding sugar to her cup.

"Orlando's story."

Sarah grabbed a stirring straw and stuck it in her cup. "It's very likely. I mean, everything he says fits. Obviously, we interpreted his intentions wrong in those letters."

Adam rubbed his chin. "Yeah, but he could be playing off the daddy issues. You know, reframing it."

"True, but I don't see it," Sarah said, stirring the cream into her hot beverage. "He seems genuine about how he feels about Rufus and his dad. It makes sense that, after his dad died, he would want to reconnect with Rufus."

"I still think he's playing us."

Sarah grabbed a chair to pull it out and took a seat. "What about Judy?"

"What about her?"

"What if she lied?" Sarah asked. "How does she not know that Orlando Prince is a long-time best friend of Rufus?"

"Maybe he didn't tell her."

Sarah narrowed her eyes. "I don't know. Maybe."

"Look," Adam said. "I held you here long enough. Why don't you and Emma go home? Have some dinner with Grandpa Larry."

Sarah nodded in agreement. She was exhausted after waking up in the wee hours of the morning, and after all the excitement and running, waiting, and watching an interrogation, she was more tired than hungry. Though, she knew Grandpa wouldn't allow her to go to bed on an empty stomach if he could help it. Besides, she couldn't wait to get out of the candy cane clothes.

"You want to join us for dinner?" she asked Adam.

"No, I'm going to stay here and finish gathering statements from the last of the Santas. But I'll walk you and Emma out."

Adam led the way out the door and down the hall to the room Emma was in with Officer Finley, where she was giving her statement. After about another ten minutes of waiting, Emma was released out of the room, and Adam escorted them back out to the door that led to the waiting area.

When Adam opened the door, they could hear commotion at Officer Deats's desk. At first, Sarah thought it was the Grinch, finally fed up with waiting, but she recognized the voices.

"I heard you had him in custody," Davey said. "I'm going back there." He sidestepped to get around Deats's desk to the door.

Deats, who was now standing, puffed up his chest. "I can't allow that, sir."

"But he killed my brother." Davey tried to maneuver around the desk again.

Deats put his hand out to the man's chest, blocking him. "If I have to, I will restrain you."

Buster stormed through the front door of the police station with Houdini at his side, followed by Judy and Faith. Everyone in the waiting area, including the three Santas, the gingerbread man, the Grinch, and the Christmas tree, swiveled their heads toward the door, enduring the dramatics of another chaotic incident.

"Davey! What are you doing?" Buster asked. Houdini, the Jack Russell terrier, yipped, matching his sentiments.

Davey whipped his head around and strolled up to Buster. "Don't you know? They got the guy that killed our brother. But they won't let me see him."

"Why do you want to see him?" Buster asked.

"I want him to tell me why he did it."

"Oh, Davey," Judy cooed. She walked up to him. Her forehead crinkled with sadness and understanding. "I'm sure the police are doing everything they can. Let's leave them to their jobs." She took him by the shoulders and led him to the door. When they passed Houdini, he let out a low grumble.

"Houdini!" Buster said, giving the red leash a short tug. The Jack Russell whined, hanging his head slightly. Buster regarded Officer Deats. "Sorry, he's in unfamiliar territory."

"Yeah, well," Deats said, pointing to the dog, "we don't allow dogs in here."

"Really? Don't you have police dogs?"

Deats put his hands on his hips, eyeing the man and the dog. "Of course, we do. But *he's* not allowed in here."

Adam stepped forward. "Officer Deats—it's okay."

Deats folded his arms across his chest. "If we allow him in here, then everyone will start bringing their dogs."

"It's harmless," Adam said.

Buster took a step back. "I didn't mean to bring him. It's just that Faith and Judy found me just up the street, walking Houdini, and they told me that they'd heard about this Orlando guy being apprehended on the news. I assumed he came here for answers."

"Well, he should have stayed home and waited for us to speak with all of you," Adam said.

"So, you did catch him?"

"We're questioning a man who might have been involved, but that is all I can tell you for now."

Buster dropped his gaze to the floor. "I understand. We'll go now."

"We'll call you when we have more information," Adam added.

"Thank you, sir," Buster said. He turned to the door and walked out, Houdini trailing behind him.

Adam let out a sigh. "Officer Deats, can you pull up the news on the computer?"

"Sure thing." Deats started clacking on the keyboard, while Sarah, Adam, and Emma stood behind him. The first headline was, "Surfing Santas Now a Santa Shake Down."

Adam brought his fingers to either side of his head, rubbing his temples. "Oh, brother."

Deats turned around. "Sheriff isn't going to be too happy to see this."

"Deats," Adam said, pulling his hands down his face. "You're not helping."

Deats swiveled his chair back around to the computer.

"Hey, looks like there's a video," Emma said. She pointed to the big box on the screen that had a play button. "Click on that."

Sarah groaned internally. The last thing she wanted to see was raw video of her running, especially in a candy cane outfit.

The people in the waiting area were now all on their phones, and Sarah could already hear the distant audio of Adam yelling, mixed with the sounds of whoever had filmed the escapade with their phone talking and laughing.

Deats clicked on the video, and it began to play.

There were two news anchors, a thirty-year-old blonde woman and a man who seemed to be at least ten years her senior.

The woman spoke: "That's right, Bob, apparently the annual Surfing Santas event turned 'naughty' when a man was chased down by not only Santa, but his little helpers, too. Cindy Appleton has the story."

The video then showed a split screen, the two anchors on one side and a smiling woman with dark curly hair on the other. She was standing on the beach with a microphone and an earpiece.

"Thank you, Mary," Cindy said. Then she took up the rest of the screen. "Moments ago, a man was apprehended at the Surfing Santas event. He was chased down by one of Cascade Cove's police officers, who was dressed up as Santa…"

The shot on the screen cut to raw footage taken with a shaky camera that showed Orlando Prince in his tweed suit running, while Santa was several feet behind him, yelling for him to "wait" and "stop."

Then Yukon Cornelius was on the screen with his red earmuffs and axe. "Yeah, I saw a bunch of people chasing this man. I figured maybe someone had been mugged or something, but I didn't see a purse in his hands. So, I didn't know what was going on."

The camera panned back to Cindy, the reporter on

the beach. "And just as Santa and his little helpers were about to lose the man, one of the surfing Santas swooped in and tackled him."

Raw footage from a different angle showed Teek coming in off a wave and intercepting the man. Teek, now close and with a microphone aimed toward him, was on screen. "Dude, I was just surfin' and saw this dude runnin'. And my bro is a detective and was chasing him. I knew somethin' was up. So, like, there was this killer wave comin' in and I just scootched into the pocket, and I boogied on down the line." Teek used his hand to show how he had gone straight down the middle. "And then, wham! I slammed it off the top. I mean, you should have seen it! Buckets, dude!" He paused a moment. "I mean, dudette." Teek chuckled, nodding his head. "It was totally righteous!" he added, grinning ear to ear.

"Uh, thanks," Cindy said, though it was more like a question. She turned back to the camera. Teek was behind her, giving two thumbs up and waving. "Well, you heard him, folks, it was 'totally righteous.' Back to you, Bob and Mary."

Adam huffed in frustration. "I've seen enough," he said. "Turn it off."

Officer Deats clicked out of the video, and Adam's cell phone rang. When he glanced at the screen, he paused, took a deep breath, and whispered to Sarah, "It's the sheriff."

Officer Deats's eyes went wide. "Oh boy."

Adam put the phone to his ear and said, "Hello."

Sarah could hear the sheriff's voice all the way over from where she stood. "What in tarnation is going on? Here I am, about to have dinner with my family, and what do I see on the TV but you and a whole Christmas village chasing after a man. What a circus. You better have a good explanation for all of this, Detective Dunkin!"

"Sir, I swear," Adam said into his phone, "I have everything under control."

"You better! And those Shores girls better not be there!"

"No, no. Sir, I will fix this."

Adam took the phone from his ear and shoved it in his pocket. "Look, you guys better go. I'll catch up with you later. The sheriff is having a conniption."

"Good idea," Sarah said.

The Grinch stood. "Does this mean I can go, too?"

Adam put his fingers to his temples again and groaned.

CHAPTER 17

Sarah and Emma began their trek home, and Sarah hoped that Adam would be able straighten everything out for Sheriff Wheeler. She didn't want Adam in hot water, yet again.

"I can't believe it," Emma said. She had an extra spring in her step that Sarah didn't quite understand. How could she still have any energy left? "What a day!"

"Yeah, you weren't kidding when you said that this would be an event I would never forget."

Emma laughed. "Well, now with the bad guy behind bars, we can enjoy a nice, quiet Christmas."

"I don't think it was Orlando."

"Wait," Emma said. "You don't think it was your mystery guy? But you said that he was the most suspicious person surrounding this case."

"That was when I thought he took off out of town, but he didn't. He hung around."

"A lot of murderers like to be close to the case, lend a helping hand to the police."

It was true that there were many instances in which the murderer remained in plain sight. In fact, sometimes they seemed more than accommodating in helping police solve the case—either to veer the police in the wrong direction or to see how close they were to being busted. But Sarah couldn't think of anyone who had been going above and beyond to help in this case—except Judy. She'd been holding her family back when they had outbursts, telling them to let the police do their job. But was that the same thing? Sarah shook her head. "It's not that."

"What is it, then?"

"Were we watching the same interrogation today? You saw how distraught he was."

"He ran from the police."

"You heard him. You'd do the same thing if you saw a mob of people chasing after you."

Emma let out a breath. "But he doesn't even have an alibi."

"True. At least, not yet."

Placing her hands on her hips, Emma cocked her head. "Only you could watch a person's behavior and demeanor and conclude whether they're lying, even when they're clearly shedding crocodile tears."

"You don't believe me?"

"No. That's the problem. I believe you, even though I don't agree with you." Emma shook her head in disbelief.

"I'm not saying that Orlando Prince is completely off the hook as a suspect. I'm just saying that I don't think he's lying, either."

Emma pursed her lips. "I don't know, Sarah. He's got a lot against him right now."

They started walking again. It had been a long day, and the sun was already hanging low in the sky, casting a warm glow over Cascade Cove.

When they reached Larry's Pawfect Boutique, they made their way straight to the apartment they lived in above the shop. Rugby greeted them with extra-sloppy kisses, while Winston sat patiently, his big ears perked up, and wiggled with excitement. Misty, on the other hand, was on the back of the sofa. She rolled over onto her back, stretching and purring. Misty would saunter over when she felt like it.

"Good!" Grandpa Larry said, as he appeared in the doorway of the living room. "You're both home. I want to show you something."

Both Sarah and Emma groaned in unison.

"Grandpa, can't it wait?" Emma whined. "I'm tired." She craned her neck to see if there was food being made in the kitchen. "Did you make anything? I'm starving."

"I'll get to that," Larry said. "But first, I've been working on a magic trick, and I finally got it." He motioned to the couch and the La-Z-Boy. "Go on, sit!" he said, before scurrying into the other room.

Emma plopped down on the couch and huffed, blowing a long strand of blonde hair out of her face. "The one time he doesn't make food."

"Give him a break," Sarah said, taking a seat on the recliner. "He's going through a lot. Especially with his favorite magician now dead."

Moments later, Larry reappeared dressed up in a magician's outfit, complete with a top hat, dragging a folding table into the room. Once he had the table in position, he pulled out a black tablecloth and opened it. He placed it over the table, adjusting it so that it was even in the middle.

When he finally had everything in place, he took his position behind the table. "Okay, girls, you ready?"

Sarah and Emma nodded.

"Great!" Larry took off his top hat. "So, you see there is nothing in my hat?" He collapsed the hat and opened it again.

"Yes, Grandpa," Emma said. "We see that it's empty."

"Good!" Larry picked up his magic wand and began waving it around the hat, which was now sitting on the table in front of him. After a few magic words, he gave the hat's brim one quick whack. "And Presto!"

Larry stuck his hand into the hat. He let out a nervous giggle. "Hold on, girls," he said, his hand now fumbling inside the hat. Finally, he took his hand out and tipped the hat upside down, before looking inside.

Then Sarah spotted something green and round slowly crawling on the floor behind Larry's magic table. Sarah pointed to the little creature creeping away. "Grandpa? Is that what you're looking for?"

Emma jumped up, cradling her legs under her on the couch so the creature couldn't get her. "Woah! What is that?"

The turtle paused at Emma's cries and craned its neck to get a look at her.

Misty hissed as Rugby crept up toward the little guy, sniffing. The turtle acknowledged him and then carried on, crawling slowly to its destination—wherever that was. When it moved, Rugby jumped back with a yelp and ran behind the couch.

"Rugby!" Sarah said. "It's just a turtle!"

Larry picked up the turtle. "There you are! You got away from me."

"Where on Earth did you get that thing?" Emma said. Her body was crammed in between the couch cushions.

Larry pulled out a spinach leaf from his pocket and gave it to the turtle.

"His name is Herbie. He's Mr. Fudderman's turtle. He said I could pet-sit him tonight, and I thought he would be perfect for my magic trick, rather than a rabbit or a dove. Isn't he perfect?"

"No!" Emma cried. "We don't have room for any…reptiles."

Sarah laughed. "Are you seriously afraid of a little turtle?"

"I'm not afraid. I just don't like it."

Sarah cocked her head to one side. "Sort of like how I don't like spiders or heights."

"All right," Emma said. "I get it."

Sarah grinned, knowing she had won.

"That's okay," Larry said, hiding the turtle in his top hat, which was sitting upside down on the magician's table. "I have another trick."

Emma groaned. "Not another one, Grandpa. I think I am all magicked out for the night."

"This one's a good one. I just need an assistant. Would either one of my beautiful granddaughters like to assist me?"

"No way!" Emma said, shaking her head vigorously. "Not if there is another reptile involved."

Larry regarded Sarah. "What about you?"

Sarah put her finger to her chin. "A beautiful assistant," Sarah said, her voice trailing off.

"That's right!" Larry said, holding out his hand, waiting.

Sarah turned to Emma. "A beautiful assistant."

"Yeah?" Emma said, motioning toward their grandfather. "Have at it."

Sarah shook her head. "No. Remember that man who came to the shop the other day? The big guy named Atticus?"

Emma thought a moment. "Oh, that guy. I could never forget him."

"Remember what he said about magicians? That they all had to have—"

"A beautiful assistant," Emma said, completing Sarah's thought.

"So, who was Rufus's assistant?"

Emma pulled out her phone. After a few taps, she handed Sarah the device.

On the screen was a gorgeous young woman with long, dark hair, curled and pinned, wearing a skimpy black outfit with red stiletto heels. Sarah scrolled down. Under the picture was a name.

"Bebe Binkerton," Sarah said out loud.

Larry scratched his head. It was clear he didn't understand what they were talking about.

Sarah jumped up and gave her confused grandpa a kiss on the cheek. "Thanks, Grandpa."

She was just about out of the room when she heard Larry giggle and say, "You're welcome."

CHAPTER 18

The next day, Sarah was on her way to Patricia's Tea Room. She'd spoken to Adam about Bebe Binkerton, Rufus's assistant, the night before. He'd told her that they were meaning to talk with her, but that he didn't have time since chasing down Orlando Prince, whom he still had in custody. Sarah told him that she would try to talk to Bebe as soon as she could. After talking to several old friends from town, she'd learned that Bebe was frequenting one of Sarah and Adam's favorite places to nibble on treats and sip hot beverages—Patricia's Tea Room.

Sarah strolled through the door, the familiar jingle of the bells above the door and the sweet smell of fresh pastries leaving her elated.

"Sarah!" Patricia called out from behind the counter.

She had her arms out to either side as she wove through the tables to greet Sarah with a big bear hug. "So nice to see you again."

"I'm glad to see you're still doing well," Sarah said, returning Patricia's embrace.

"Healthy as a horse!"

"And noisier than a chorus frog," Nancy said as she was passing by, hauling two mugs to one of the front tables.

Patricia flapped her hand. "Don't listen to her. She's just jealous that I've been getting much of the attention around here."

"I'm not jealous," Nancy said, after delivering the drink order. She wiped her hands on her apron and took her nana's hand. "I'm glad. It's nice to see you back to your old self again."

Patricia smiled. "Oh, honey. Thank you." She let go of her granddaughter's hand. "Now we just have to find you an eligible bachelor."

"Oh, Nana," Nancy said. "Don't start."

Patricia turned to Sarah. "How about you? You nab Adam Dunkin yet?"

Hands on her hips, Nancy shook her head. "I'm sorry," she said to Sarah. "I don't know what has gotten into her lately."

"Sorry for what?" Patricia asked. "Love is beautiful

and worth waking up to. You'd both know that if you'd stop pretending that you don't need it." Patricia's eyes glazed over in reverie. "I remember the first time I laid eyes on your grandfather."

"Oh, brother," Nancy said, rolling her eyes.

Patricia ignored her granddaughter's remark. "It was 1959 and I was in college, leaving my English Lit class—and there he was." Her trance broke, and she regarded both of the young women who stood before her. "I was like you two. Determined to make something of myself. But it was love at first sight. An unspoken bond that could never be broken. We married four weeks later."

"Four weeks later!" Nancy said, eyes wide. She lowered her voice to a whisper, her eyebrows wrinkled in curiosity. "Nana, did you get pregnant?"

"No, of course not! It's called love. You'd know if you'd take a break once in a while. Get out, bask in the sun, smell the flowers..." Patricia leaned into her granddaughter, shielding her mouth with her hand. "Bump into a nice gentleman," she added, waggling her eyebrows.

Sarah giggled.

"Nana, you're too much," Nancy said, swatting her grandmother's shoulder gently. She glanced at Sarah. "So, are you here for another order of key lime bars?"

"Just a cup of chamomile tea would be lovely," Sarah said.

"Sure thing," Nancy said. "I'll get that for you right away. Why don't you take that table over there." She pointed to a table that was next to the one she and Adam had sat at a few days before, in the back corner.

"Thank you," Sarah said, before making her way to her seat.

The petite elderly woman followed her. "I heard they captured the murderer."

Sarah pulled out a chair and took a seat. "Well, they have a person of interest in custody."

"So, they're not the murderer?" Patricia joined her at the table, sitting across from her.

Sarah shrugged. "Could be. Could not be. Like I said, he's a person of interest."

"But didn't he do it?"

"They don't know," Sarah said.

"But—"

Sarah smiled, taking Patricia's hand and covering it with her other hand. "We will find who did this. You don't need to worry."

"Oh, sweetie, I'm not worried. I heard it was personal."

Sarah furrowed her eyebrows. "Where did you hear that?"

"Well, I didn't. I just heard that someone bumped him over the head. You know, by the old Beachside Beacon." Patricia leaned back into her chair. "I don't know about you, but being hit over the head with a rock sounds pretty personal to me. And if it's personal, then that means the person isn't a serial murderer."

Sarah's mouth hung open for a moment before she realized it. Everything Patricia had said was true, and she didn't need the reassurance that she was safe in her neighborhood. And if that was the case, maybe Patricia could help her.

Sarah took a deep breath. "I need to ask you something."

"Go ahead," Patricia said. "I'll answer to the best of my knowledge."

Sarah grinned. She had to admit, the woman was endearing. "Have you seen a woman in your tea room who is tall with long black hair, ironed and curled, with green eyes? You really couldn't miss her. She's modelesque."

"Why, yes. Sounds like you're describing Bebe. She's been coming here every day for the past week at about noon. Why?"

Sarah was shocked by how easy this was. Though, she shouldn't have been. Patricia had a great memory and knew all her customers by name, usually privy to all the gossip that surrounded each patron.

"No reason. I just know that she's new in town."

"New in town?" Patricia arched an eyebrow. "Didn't you know? She's been Rufus's assistant the past few years. Though, come to think of it, she didn't seem too choked up about Rufus's passing."

Sarah wondered why she hadn't come to Patricia sooner. She seemed to have the scoop on everybody.

"Though I shouldn't speak ill of her," Patricia continued. "She's been a star customer. Giving us large tips every day. She should be popping in any time now."

The bells above the door chimed again, and Patricia got up from her chair. "I should help Nancy."

Sarah smiled with understanding.

"And don't forget what I said before about finding love. I see how you look at Adam Dunkin."

"I don't look at him—"

Patricia put her hand up, stopping Sarah mid-sentence. "He's got eyes for you, too," Patricia continued. "Love can be so deep and strong. It doesn't always give you a choice. And when you finally surrender to it, it'll be so glorious and blissful—you'll do anything for each other."

Patricia left, greeting the new customers. Sarah just

sat there with her mouth hanging open. Had she been that obvious around Adam?

Nancy waltzed over, delivering not only the hot tea Sarah had ordered, but a sticky bun topped with pecans.

"On the house," Nancy said with a smile as she placed the delicious treat in front of Sarah, breaking into her thoughts. The sweet aroma wafted up, and Sarah salivated. She devoured the mouthwatering sticky bun within minutes, and ordered another. How could she not? Between the anxiety of finding Bebe Binkerton and the speech Patricia had given her about Adam and love, she couldn't help herself. Besides, after all the calories she'd burned from chasing Orlando, she could easily justify the extra sticky bun treat.

She popped the last sweet morsel into her mouth and looked at the clock. If Bebe arrived at noon every day, she'd have to wait another hour. She pulled out her phone and gave Adam an update. Then she tapped on a dice game she'd downloaded onto her phone months ago to kill time. She leaned back into her chair, stretching her legs out as she played. It wasn't exactly Yahtzee, but it was similar enough that if anyone had played that popular game, they'd have an idea of the point system.

After several rounds of her game, the bells jingled at the entrance. Sarah glanced up involuntarily. She straightened herself in her chair when she saw the tall, dark-haired woman enter the tea room. She had green eyes and the most beautiful complexion Sarah had ever seen.

Under her breath, Sarah muttered, “Bebe Binkerton.”

CHAPTER 19

Bebe Binkerton's black stilettos click-clacked against the vinyl wood flooring as she made her way to the counter and placed her order before finding an open table. She had a magazine in hand, and she paged through it as she waited for her tea or food to be delivered.

Sarah approached the woman, trying not to let her nerves get the best of her. The woman seemed rather intimidating, and Sarah didn't know if it was because of her flawless beauty, her tall stature, or perhaps Bebe simply had an aura that was unsettling to her.

Sarah cleared her throat. "Excuse me."

Bebe glanced up from her magazine. "Yes?" she asked, her green eyes boring into Sarah's. "Can I help you with something?" Her eyes were hypnotizing.

"Are you Bebe Binkerton?"

The woman raised her eyebrows. "Who's asking?"

Sarah sat down across from the woman, a daring move. "My name is Sarah Shores. Big fan of Rufus and you."

"You want an autograph or something?" Bebe reached for her purse.

"No. That isn't necessary. See—"

Patricia strolled up to the table. "Bebe Binkerton. I see you met Sarah Shores. She's investigating Rufus's murder."

"Oh, is she?" Bebe gazed into Sarah's eyes. She propped her elbows on the table, resting her chin in her hands. "Please, go on."

Sarah couldn't believe Patricia had blown her cover like that.

Sarah scoffed. "No. That's not entirely true. I mean, I'm not the police or anything."

Bebe grinned. "So, you're a detective?" She narrowed her eyes. "Private investigator?"

"No." Sarah waved her words away. "None of that. I work at a pet boutique on the boardwalk with my grandfather. I'm just a fan of Rufus's work."

"Don't underestimate yourself, Sarah," Patricia said. She regarded Bebe. "She works with Adam Dunkin. He's a very intuitive detective who—"

"Patricia," Sarah said, interrupting her. "Would you be a dear and get me another cup of chamomile tea?"

Patricia paused. "Oh. Uh, surely," she said, giving Sarah a wink.

Sarah smiled back at Patricia as she sauntered away to retrieve her order.

"Isn't she endearing?" Sarah said. She whirled a finger in a circular motion by her ear. "Wild imagination, though."

Bebe nodded, her eyes still glued to Sarah's in skepticism.

She had to think quickly. Then she remembered one of Orlando's letters that mentioned an admirable magic trick. A trick she'd seen before in Vegas.

"Anyway, as I was saying, I loved the trick he did where he sawed a woman in half, put her back together, then made her disappear! It was like an homage to the McFreed and Floyd act in Vegas."

"It's wasn't an homage. Rufus came up with that routine himself, before McFreed and Floyd stole it. They should have stuck to their little cats."

"You mean lions?"

"Whatever. Look, Sandra—"

"Sarah," she corrected.

Bebe stared at her for a moment. "Sarah. I don't know who you are, but I can tell you this. Whatever you think about the Hattingsfords, you are probably wrong. Sure, Rufus could be rough around the edges, and he certainly did questionable things to get ahead in his career. But he is not entirely at fault for his sandpaper personality. No one in that family is who you think they are."

"What about Buster? He seems nice."

"Buster is a leech. He never left his brother's house to make a life of his own. The family's unfortunate crudeness dates back generations. The only kind person to ever enter into their lives was Orlando Prince's father, who took them under his wing and made Rufus who he was."

"I heard about that. He taught Rufus and Buster everything about magic."

"He sure did, and he did everything to bond the boys forever. He gave them each a gold ring with an emerald gem. He said it would not only bond them in brotherhood but bestow great fortune upon them all. Rufus cherished his ring and never took it off, as did his brothers."

Sarah recalled the ring Buster was twirling the day they found Rufus's body. "Rings?"

Bebe locked eyes with Sarah. "Fourteen carat, pure yellow-gold rings with two white diamonds on either side of the emerald gem. When I say he took these boys under his wing, I mean, he took good care of them. Each one of those rings is a mini-fortune in itself."

Sarah's eyes went wide.

"Anyway," Bebe continued. "After the funeral, I will be gone with the wind. Far from his wife, his sister-in-law, and Buster."

"Where will you go?" Sarah asked.

"I got a call from my agent. I'll be auditioning for a show in New York."

"Broadway?"

Bebe shook her head. "Dancer. Now, if you'll excuse me," she said, getting up from her seat, "I'd like to enjoy my last days here in Florida before I fly back north into the bitter cold."

Sarah shivered at the mention of New York winters.

"Oh, and Sandra," Bebe said, turning around, "don't let the investigation run too long. I only have a few days to spare before auditions are closed." She took her sunglasses from her head and placed them over her eyes before making her way out the door, her stilettos clacking.

Sarah froze. Who was this woman? And why did she keep calling her Sandra?

Patricia arrived with an ivory teacup and saucer decorated with pink pansies. "Interesting character," she said, before placing the tea down in front of Sarah.

"Sure is," Sarah said, still staring at the door Bebe had exited.

"You think she was behind the murder?"

Sarah shook her head. "I don't know."

Patricia nodded. "Would you like another sticky bun?"

"Oh, good heavens, no," Sarah said, clutching her stomach.

"Suit yourself," Patricia said, walking away.

Sarah opened her purse and dug out her cell phone. She had to call Adam and let him know what she'd learned. When he answered, she relayed the entire conversation to him.

"Thanks for trying, Sarah," he said. "But I think we already have our murderer in custody."

"Orlando? I still think he was set up."

"He has motive, means, and opportunity."

"He doesn't remember where he was that night."

"He claims he was asleep," Adam said. Sarah could hear Adam rifling through his notes. When the ruffling of papers stopped, he added, "He said that he went to bingo and left at nine. Then he drove straight to his motel, watched some TV before falling asleep. Which means he doesn't have an alibi."

"Why didn't he just say that before?"

"Because he didn't remember exactly what night he

did what, and he didn't want to lie to the police. He wanted to be sure of his whereabouts."

"So what makes you think it was him?"

"He's a liar."

Sarah palmed her forehead. "You just said that he didn't want to lie to the police."

"That's what he says. But get this. When I asked him if he knew Davey Hattingsford, he said yes, and that he'd run into him the day of Rufus's murder."

"But he couldn't have. Davey didn't arrive to Cascade Cove until after his brother's murder."

"Exactly," Adam said. "We were there ourselves when he arrived at the Hattingsfords' beach house."

Sarah let out a long breath. Something wasn't adding up. "So, what did he say about his relationship with Davey?"

"Well, they went to the same college. Though, Orlando was a senior and Davey was a freshman. Orlando said that Davey followed him around. Wanted to get with the girls like Orlando did."

"So, he looked up to him."

"Sort of," Adam said. "Until one night, there was a party, and Orlando was supposed to set Davey up with a girl that he had eyes for. But Rufus crashed those plans when he showed up unannounced."

"Rufus didn't go to the college?" Sarah asked.

"Nope. He didn't go to college at all. He had a magician's career he was building. So, Rufus got there, and the girl arrived. Davey was upstairs, getting himself ready and working up the guts to go talk to this girl. When he came down to join the party, he found Rufus with her, pulling a red carnation from her ear."

"Oh boy," Sarah said.

"'Oh boy' is right," Adam said. "Davey was distraught."

"So, what does this have to do with anything?"

"Nothing much, except for the girl."

"What about her?" Sarah asked.

"It was Judy."

CHAPTER 20

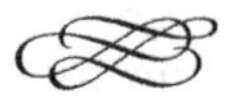

Sarah made her way back to the boutique, her mind whirling. When she walked through the door, Winston waddled over to greet her, while Rugby clumsily galloped toward her, eager to get a vigorous scratch behind the ears. Sarah accommodated both dogs.

"Hey, Sarah," Emma said, wiping the counter with a rag. Her phone buzzed in her back pocket and she pulled it out. With a grin, she tapped the screen a few times, probably texting someone.

"Is that Mark?" Sarah asked.

"Yeah, he's just telling me how his Great-Aunt Althea is getting tipsy at his parents' dinner party. Letting a few family secrets spill, apparently." Emma put her phone away with a giggle. Sarah loved seeing her cousin so happy.

"Miss Mark, don't you?"

Emma shrugged dismissively. "Well, just the part where I get to hound him on a daily basis."

Sarah chuckled. "Don't you do that anyway, over the phone?"

"It's not the same."

"I'm sure he misses you, too."

"He'll be back after Christmas," Emma said matter-of-factly, continuing to dust the counter. "So, did you meet the beautiful assistant, Bebe Binkerton?"

Sarah nodded.

"So? Learn any new information?" Emma asked.

"Not really."

Emma frowned. "That's too bad. I thought she'd have something useful."

Sarah let out a long breath. "Nothing about this murder makes sense, and we haven't eliminated anyone. This one is really a mystery, and I don't think I'll be able to solve it."

Emma dropped the rag and sashayed around the counter, putting her arm around Sarah. "First off, you don't need to solve every murder. That would be insane. And secondly, if this murder can be solved, I'd put all my money on you to solve it."

Sarah glanced at her cousin and smiled warmly. "Thanks."

"Now," Emma said, picking up the rag and tossing it in a box behind the counter, "if you are determined to solve this, I think it's best we first review all of the suspects."

Sarah nodded.

Emma leaned on the counter. "Okay, so our first suspect is Buster, who had just found out that his brother was the one who sabotaged his magician career. He doesn't have an alibi for the twenty-minute window in which his brother was killed."

"Correct," Sarah said.

"We also have Orlando Prince."

"I don't think he did it, Em."

Emma shrugged. "The evidence points to him. His mysterious lurking around town, and the red handkerchief with his initials sewn on it, found in the victim's hand."

"I understand, but it seems too easy. Like it was a setup."

"Fair enough," Emma said. "What about his wife? The spouse is always the first suspect, and Judy would gain a fortune with him dead. He left just about everything to her."

"Yes, but I think that was out of convenience. He

knew she'd share it with his brother, Buster, and her sister, Faith—not to mention, Houdini, whom Buster takes care of anyway. Besides, they ruled her out early in the investigation."

"Perhaps too early? She doesn't have a solid alibi. Faith can't vouch that she was in bed that night."

"Though, Judy also can't vouch for her sister, Faith, either."

"Maybe they were in on it together?"

Sarah hadn't thought of that. "Maybe I should run that theory by Adam."

"I think you should. Who would want him dead?" Emma tapped her finger to her chin. "His assistant, Bebe Binkerton?"

"No, she had nothing to gain."

"Could have been revenge. Or what about the mother and son who were in the store the day Rufus died?"

"Possible, but unlikely."

"I agree, though it's not impossible."

"True." Sarah bit her lip. "What's impossible is this mystery."

Emma dropped her shoulders. "Look, why don't you just take a break from the case and help me in the shop?" The corner of Emma's mouth ticked up. "I could use the company, and there's a lot of inventory to count."

"I don't know."

Emma bent down and retrieved the old rag she'd been using to dust and threw it at Sarah. It hit her shoulder, close enough to her face.

"Hey!"

"Stop being a poop and help me."

Sarah laughed. "All right, all right."

Emma pointed to the other side of the room. "Start on those shelves." Then she went over to the radio and blasted a Bing Crosby song.

Sarah got to work helping her cousin dust before helping count inventory, turning down the music every time a customer entered the store. But the peppy Christmas music made them happy and energetic, which in turn made the customers happy.

After several hours of the cleaning party, they started on inventory. Emma was right: counting inventory was incredibly monotonous and boring after only a few minutes. The last few hours passed slower than Herbie, the turtle.

Emma looked at the clock. "Closing time. You want me to help you lock up?"

Sarah waved her away. "No, it's your day off. You go. I got this."

"All right." Emma grabbed Misty from the shelf and placed the cat on her shoulder as she made her way to the door that led to the apartment upstairs. She called for Winston and Rugby. Winston sauntered out from behind the counter as Rugby came out of Larry's office, stretching from his evening, pre-dinner nap. "Let's go, guys." Emma led them up the steps, shutting the door behind her.

Sarah locked the front door and flipped the sign from "Open" to "Closed." Then she went to the front window where the Christmas dog was displayed and unplugged it. Each corner of the place grew dark as she unplugged more of the Christmas lights.

She was about to turn off the Christmas tree when she heard a dog yip. It was a familiar bark, but she knew immediately it wasn't one of her dogs.

She paused. After a few moments, she proceeded to unplug the Christmas tree. She was on her hands and knees looking for the plug when she heard the dog yip again. Was it coming from outside?

Sarah got up and tip-toed to the front entrance to take a peek. She cupped her hands around her eyes, shielding the reflection of the inside lights to get a better look. Her nose touched the cool glass, and that's when she saw him.

"Houdini?"

CHAPTER 21

The little Jack Russell bounced slightly with each bark. He stopped when he saw Sarah.

Sarah unlocked the glass door to the boutique and opened it a crack.

"Houdini," she said. "What are you doing here all by yourself? Where's Buster?"

He let out another bark. Sarah took a step toward the dog, and he backed up.

"I'm sure Buster is worried about you." Sarah tried to move toward the dog again, but this time slowly. He backed away, keeping a few feet between them, though he stared at her like he wanted to tell her something.

"Stay," Sarah said. She lunged quickly to catch him, but the dog took off running, and Sarah hurried after him.

"Houdini!" she shouted. The little Jack Russell scurried down the boardwalk, his nails clicking rapidly on the wooden boards.

"Houdini!" she yelled. "Stay!" But he only ran faster. Sarah couldn't believe it. She'd gotten more exercise in the past two days than she had the entire year. She only hoped no one was recording her on their phone this time to broadcast on the news.

It wasn't long before she realized they had passed Jacobs Manor and the pier. Was he running back home? Sarah wasn't sure but wanted to keep the dog in her sights just in case. She was glad she did, because they were now going past the Hattingsfords' house. Then Houdini took a turn toward the Beachside Beacon. When he arrived at the Beacon, he stopped right outside the door and began springing up and down. Sarah turned around to see the Hattingsfords' house. The lights were on, and four silhouettes could be seen through the dining room sliding-glass doors—two men and two women. She recognized Judy and Davey right away, but the other man wasn't Buster. This guy was much bigger, and the woman had long hair, not short curly hair that was usually tied up in a bun like Faith's. Sarah inched closer toward the house to get a better look, but she couldn't make out who the other two people were. She turned her attention back to the springing dog.

"What are you doing?" Sarah said in a harsh whisper, though her voice was lost in the roar of the crashing waves hitting the rocks on the terrain next to them.

Houdini stopped jumping and began scratching at the wooden door, whining. He looked back at Sarah with his dark, round eyes. Sarah approached the door slowly. She couldn't see much in the dark, but she could tell that the latch was rusted. Houdini whined, glancing up at her again.

"All right, all right," Sarah said, though she was still wary about opening it. She'd assumed that the old Beachside Beacon would be locked—but concluded that it used to be locked, when her foot kicked something hard. She bent down and picked up an old, corroded padlock.

"Stay here," she said to Houdini, who was alert, with his ears perked. She wasn't sure what good that would do, since he didn't seem to listen to anyone, including Buster and the late Mr. Hattingsford.

Sarah grasped the cold metal handle of the door and opened the door a crack, peering around it. It was pitch black inside. She pulled out her cell phone to use the flashlight feature on the device, shining it around the room. The place was so old and dingy, smelling like a musty basement.

Houdini nudged his head between Sarah's ankles to get a look himself and let out a small yip that echoed in the large, cold lung of the Beacon.

Sarah looked down at Houdini. "Shh." The last thing she needed right now was for anyone to hear her or the dog while snooping around near the crime scene, especially when the murderer was still on the loose.

A gust of wind whipped Sarah's locks, and the hairs on her neck stood. Nope, she thought, closing the door in front of her. She couldn't go inside the dark Beacon. Not without backup. She turned off the flashlight on her phone and gave her screen a few more taps before bringing it to her ear.

After a few rings, Adam picked up with a hello that lifted some of Sarah's anxiety.

"Adam, could you meet me over at the old Beachside Beacon?"

"Sarah, I'm kind of in the middle of something."

"Whatever it is, I'm sure it's not as important as this. Houdini got loose and is at the Beacon. He's scratching and whining to go in."

"Oh, you're right, Sarah. Apprehending a loose dog, who's practically in his own backyard, is definitely more important than nabbing a murderer."

Sarah pursed her lips. "Just get down here, and quick. I think the dog is trying to show us something. He wants to go into the Beacon."

"He probably just saw some birds or something."

"Adam, I don't feel safe."

"Okay," Adam said with a huff. "I'll be there in ten."

She hung up the phone and met Houdini's puppy eyes. "Don't worry. Adam's coming." She wasn't sure if she was trying to convince the dog or herself, but either way, it made her feel better to say it out loud.

Houdini sat next to her feet as if he understood, and she gave him a pat on the head. "We're going to figure this out."

Sarah was getting cold. All she had on was a hoodie and jeans. Though they were still experiencing warm days, nights by the water always got too chilly for her. She sat with her back against the outer wall of the Beacon and her knees to her chest to keep warm. She stared out at the ocean waves that angrily slapped the boulders yards ahead from where they'd found Rufus's body just days before.

After a few minutes, Houdini lay down next to her with a huff. Patience didn't seem to be his virtue either. They waited for what felt like an eternity, until a car door slammed in the distance. Sarah stood. It sounded like it had come from the Hattingsfords' driveway. She made her way around the Beacon to take a peek. The dining room was now empty. A car started, and the glow of two headlights cut through the darkness. As the car pulled out, movement in one of the upstairs windows caught Sarah's eyes. It looked like Davey rubbing Judy's shoulders, and they were facing each other, noses almost touching. Sarah inched closer to get a better look, when a crunching footstep came from behind her. Houdini let out a low growl. She whipped around to see a shadowy figure with a flashlight standing directly behind her.

She jumped with yelp and brought her foot back for a swift, hard kick where it would count.

The man hopped back quickly. "It's just me," Adam said with his hands up.

Sarah, relieved, wiped her sweaty palms on her pants. "Finally."

"I came as quickly as I could. By the way, you should probably have mace or pepper gel on you. And you shouldn't be out here alone."

"Well, I didn't expect to be here."

Adam nodded, shining his flashlight around. "What were you looking at?"

Sarah grabbed his wrist, lowering the flashlight. "Stop shining that thing around. I just saw Judy and Davey in one of the upstairs windows."

Adam glanced up at the window, squinting. "I don't see anything."

Sarah peered back up where she had seen the two. The room was not only empty, but the lights were now off.

Houdini whined, pawing at Sarah's leg.

Adam surveyed their surroundings before he focused on the Beacon door. "I thought this was locked."

"Me too," Sarah said, holding up the old padlock.

Adam shook his head. "Teenagers, I bet."

Sarah raised her eyebrows. "Possible. But it could also be—"

"A murderer," Adam said, cutting her off. "But I'd put my money on the kids fooling around."

"Did you or the uniforms check the Beacon the day we found the body?" She already had an inkling of the answer to her question, since the crime scene tape didn't extend to the Beacon.

"I don't think so, but we assumed the murder took place at the rocky terrain," he said, pointing at the rocks that jutted out from the ground at least a dozen yards from them.

Houdini scratched the door, whining again before sitting and waiting patiently for Adam to open it.

"You weren't kidding," he said. "The little pup is eager to get inside. Probably curious."

"Yeah, well, I am too," Sarah said.

"All right. Hold your horses." Adam cracked the door a bit and put up his right hand to block Sarah from the doorway, his flashlight darting around inside the Beacon. Then, when it seemed like the coast was clear, he opened the door only wide enough for himself to slip inside. Houdini rushed in as Sarah followed up behind. Cell phone out, she turned her own flashlight on.

Adam scanned the room. "I don't see anything."

Houdini scuttled around the dilapidated Beacon, sniffing. Then he stopped on the other side and let out a yip. Sarah shined her light onto him and noticed he was standing behind something black.

He barked again. Sarah rushed over to the object, Adam on her tail. She crouched down and picked it up. "A top hat." She flipped it over and, on the inside of the brim, found a name. "Rufus."

Adam kneeled next to Sarah. "What is Rufus's hat doing in the Beacon?"

Sarah furrowed her eyebrows. "I don't know." Then something small on the ground glinted in the beam of her flashlight. Sarah handed Adam the hat, not tearing her eyes from the sparkling rock. She picked it up between her forefinger and her thumb.

"What's that?" Adam asked.

Sarah lifted it to eye level.

"An emerald gem," she said, refocusing her gaze to Adam.

"Rufus's?"

Sarah shook her head. "No, Sheriff Wheeler pointed out his ring when we found him. It still had the emerald gem." Sarah's mind was racing—suddenly, it all came together. She gasped. "I think I know who did it."

Just then, Sarah heard someone behind her at the doorway of the Beacon. "Hello?"

She instantly recognized the voice, and goosebumps prickled Sarah's arms and neck.

"Sarah, Adam. Thank you for finding Houdini," the black shadow said. Sarah could see his awkward smile even in the dark. Then he acknowledged the little dog. "Hey, little guy. How'd you get out?" The man pointed behind them, toward the house. "Time to go home."

The Jack Russell took a few steps back, letting out a low growl.

CHAPTER 22

The next day, the Florida rays flickered between the houses as Sarah stared out the window of Adam's police cruiser. It had taken Sarah a while to explain to Adam what was going on, but they had hashed out a plan, and now it was time to put that plan into action.

Adam was focused on the road. "Hope this works."

"Don't be such a pessimist, Adam," Sarah said. "Of course, it will. Besides, have I ever let you down with one of my plans before?"

Adam glanced over at her, doing a double take. "Are you serious? Twice now, you almost got yourself killed, and before that, you almost got *me* killed. Not to mention, almost fired."

"Now you're just being dramatic."

Before Sarah could reply, they pulled up to the Hattingsfords' house. It was show time.

Adam unclipped his seatbelt. "I'd tell you to stay here, but I know that's not going to happen."

Sarah paused, her seatbelt already undone and her hand on the car door's latch. "Well, I'd say you don't know me, but I guess you know more than you let on."

Adam let out a chuckle. "Just, no guns this time."

Sarah put up her hands. "I don't have any."

After a moment of silence, Adam gave her a sharp nod, finally breaking eye contact. They both opened their doors and climbed out at the same time. They made their way up the stone walkway to the stoop and rang the doorbell.

Faith opened the door, her curly blonde hair dancing in the breeze. "Officer Dunkin," she said, wrinkling her forehead. "I don't think we were expecting you today."

"Ma'am, could we come in?"

"Well, I suppose," she said, opening the door wider. Adam and Sarah walked in. "Is there something wrong?"

"Where's Mrs. Hattingsford?"

Before Faith could answer, Buster and Davey came out into the living area. "What's going on?" Buster asked.

"Sir, where is your sister-in-law?" Adam asked.

Buster's mouth fell open. "I...uh..."

Sarah heard one of the bedroom doors open, and Judy appeared around the corner.

Judy cocked her head. "Officer Dunkin...Sarah. Do you have new information?"

Adam approached her and briskly turned her around, grabbing her wrists. "Judy Hattingsford, you have the right to remain silent. Anything you say can and will be used against you in a court of law. If you—"

"What on earth do you think you're doing?" Davey asked.

Adam continued reciting the Miranda warning to Judy.

Davey's face was red with fury. "I demand an explanation!"

"We are apprehending your brother's murderer," Sarah said.

Davey's eyes went wide. "Are you insane? Judy didn't murder Rufus. How did you come to that conclusion?"

"She had motive, opportunity, and means."

"Motive? What motive?"

"She'd gain her husband's fortune. In fact, he's worth more dead than alive, especially now that he's retiring. Perfect timing, if you ask me."

Judy wiggled in the cuffs. "I didn't kill him!"

Faith's mouth hung open, her eyes darting from one person to the next. "My sister couldn't have killed him."

Davey's face burned with rage. "Are you complete morons? What about the red handkerchief? We all know it was Orlando Prince! His initials are even stitched on it!"

Sarah shook her head confidently. "No, sir. That was planted there."

"You people are insane," Davey said. "Judy didn't do anything."

Sarah stepped forward. "How can you be so sure of that, Davey? I mean, you seem awfully upset right now. I thought you'd be relieved. Don't you want us to find your brother's killer?"

"Believe me, I'm sure. She would never do anything like that." Davey's shoulders dropped and his face relaxed into admiration as he looked at Judy. "She's too sweet and kind."

"But you would," Sarah said.

Davey's eyes unlocked from Judy's. "What?"

"You would do it."

"Kill my own brother?" Davey chuckled. "Now I know you're all insane. I wasn't even in town until after he was found dead."

Now it was Sarah's turn to laugh. "We both know that's not true."

"Seriously, we all know it was Orlando Prince. The psycho stalker."

"No," Sarah said. "That's what you wanted everyone to think. You arrived here the day of your brother's murder. After Judy and Rufus left my grandfather's shop, I saw you talking with Orlando Prince. Though, I didn't recognize it was you until last night, when I saw you in the Beacon. The way you pointed behind us when you were talking to Houdini and ushering him back to the house. That's when I realized that it's not just your brothers who know magic. You, yourself, have a few tricks up your sleeve."

Davey chuckled. "And what trick is that? Teleporting?" He motioned toward Buster. "Even my big brother can't pull that one off."

Buster crossed his arms in front of his chest in irritation.

"No, Davey," Sarah said. "The sleight of hand. When you were talking to Orlando outside my grandfather's boutique the day of the murder, you pointed at something behind Orlando. That's when you swiped his handkerchief so that you could plant it at the scene of the crime."

"Oh yeah? Well, even if I did, good luck proving it."

"I saw the ring," Sarah said. "The gold ring with the emerald. The same ring your brothers Buster and Rufus have."

"Well, if what Ms. Shores is saying isn't true," Adam

said, still standing behind Judy, "I'm sure we can easily clear this up. All you'd have to do is show me your plane ticket. If there's any problem with you obtaining that ticket or information, our department can always contact the airport for you. We can clear this right up."

Davey glared at Adam. "You can't do that!"

"If you are so keen on privacy, Davey," Sarah said, "why don't you just show us the ring?" Sarah pulled out a new evidence bag from her purse and unrolled it in front of him, revealing the emerald gem.

Davey's face morphed into shock as he stammered. Then he cleared his throat, collecting himself. "I…I don't have it. I left it at home—back in New York."

Buster stepped closer, looking at his brother's hand. "You never take that ring off. Let alone, leave it miles away."

Davey motioned to his brother. "Buster, stay out of this."

"Buster's right," Faith said. "Where's the ring, Davey?"

"I swear, I lost it. I don't know where it is."

Houdini scampered in, dropping a small, heavy object at Buster's feet. Buster bent over and picked it up, his face twisted in horror. "No!" He held it up for everyone to see. The gold ring glinted in the light, though the setting where a gem should have been was empty. "How could you?"

Judy and Faith gasped.

"You don't understand," Davey stammered. "Rufus was miserable. He made all our lives miserable."

Judy's eyes went wide. "Davey!"

Davey ignored Judy. "He didn't treat Judy like she deserved. He didn't even love her."

"But you do," Sarah said.

Davey continued, "She always confided in me. It was a mistake in fate. Orlando was going to set us up in college, but Rufus came in and messed everything up. He shouldn't have even been there. We all knew that."

"But that all happened so long ago," Sarah said. "Why now?"

Davey met Sarah's eyes. "Atticus."

Sarah and Adam exchanged glances. "Atticus?" Sarah asked.

"He called me the night before I came to Cascade Cove." Davey's eyes lowered to the floor, citing the incident in reverie. "He told me that Rufus knew I loved Judy back then. He came to my college after Orlando told him that I had eyes for this girl and that he was going to set me up with her at a party. Rufus came to the party." Davey's eyes welled up. "He came to the party just to woo Judy. To take her away from me."

"But why?"

"I told you," Davey said with conviction. "He made all

our lives miserable. He had to have it all. The fame, the fortune, and the girl."

A tear rolled down Judy's face. "I'm sorry, Davey."

The silence in the room was deafening. Houdini, who sat next to Buster's feet, watched the scene unfold as if he were watching a show on TV.

Finally, Sarah spoke—a question that'd been weighing on her mind. "But why frame Orlando?"

"Because, he knew. And he allowed it to happen. He watched as Rufus wooed her with magic tricks, pulling flowers from behind her ear. He could have intervened, but he didn't."

Sarah shook her head, more confused than before. "But how did you know Orlando was here in Florida?"

"That was easy," Davey said. "My brother has been complaining for the past year that Orlando was following him. Called him a lost puppy and said that he was pathetic. Said Orlando even showed up at the house one time. So, I flew into Florida knowing that my brother comes to Cascade Cove every year at this time, and I'm walking down the boardwalk with my cap and sunglasses, trying to find my brother, and who do I run into in the process but Orlando Prince himself. He was too easy. Talking about how his father, Orlando King, died back in July and that he's been trying to contact my brother for months, but he's not answering him. I said I thought I saw him behind him, he turns around, and I take his handkerchief from his front pocket. I mean, you need evidence, right? It was a perfect plan. My brother is dead, and Orlando is framed for the murder. A perfect ending to a tragic story."

"So, you had the whole thing planned?"

"Well, not everything," Davey said. "I stayed at the Dolphin Motel just down the boardwalk, and I walked to Rufus's house. I did plan to kill him, but when I saw him, I got cold feet. I told him what Atticus told me, and he laughed. We got into an argument, and he pulled me into the Beacon. Said he didn't want to wake his wife. The argument got heated, and he shoved me. He shoved me so hard, I fell. He walked out of the Beacon, but not before he called me 'sad' and 'pathetic.' So I followed him to the rocky terrain, and I picked up a rock. And I… I…" Davey was standing there with his arms over his head, imitating what he had done that night.

"I've heard enough," Adam said, unlocking the cuffs on Judy's wrists. He walked over and placed them on Davey without effort.

Davey turned to Judy and mouthed, "I will always love you."

Judy burst into tears, her back sliding down the opposite wall from Davey. Faith crouched down to comfort her sister.

Sarah didn't know if she was crying from the horror of losing her husband or the sadness at the loss of true love. Sarah decided it was both. But one name gnawed at the back of her mind—Atticus. What was his involvement? Why was he all of a sudden revealing the ugly truth to everyone in the family about Rufus? She wasn't sure if she'd ever find out. She wasn't even sure she knew if Atticus was still in the area.

She watched as Adam shoved Davey out the door to the police cruiser as Judy's cries echoed in Sarah's head. There was more to this story, and she had to find out.

CHAPTER 23

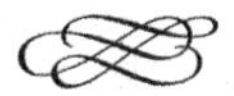

Sarah sat upright in one of the cushioned seats at the Dolphin Motel lobby, pretending to read an article, when a pair of black patent leather shoes clicked rhythmically from the elevator shaft to the front desk. She lowered her magazine to see Atticus carrying a bag and rolling a suitcase behind him.

He waved to the man standing at the front desk as he approached him. "Merry Christmas."

The man gave him a bright smile. "Only a few days away, sir."

"Yes, and I must get going before I miss my flight. Heading for the Bahama Islands for Christmas this year," he said, taking his receipt. He began heading for the door when Sarah stood up.

"Atticus," she said. "Thought you were staying for the funeral?"

Atticus glanced at her in shock. Then he looked around the room before relaxing his face. "Ah, yes. Sorry, I didn't expect the investigation to take so long. Christmas is just around the corner, and I have other obligations."

"Hm, I understand," Sarah said. "Though your name has come up several times surrounding Rufus's murder."

"Oh?"

"You know, Davey, Rufus's brother?"

Atticus shook his head. "I don't know what you're talking about."

"I heard that's what you told the police. That you didn't know Davey, but funny thing, Davey seems to know you."

Atticus pursed his lips. "No, sorry, Miss Sarah, I don't know him. Now, if you'll excuse me—"

"I saw you coming out of the Hattingsford residence last night. I was at the Beacon."

Atticus paused, thinking a moment. "Oh, yes. I was there, paying my condolences."

"Kind of late to be paying condolences, don't you think? We both know that you know exactly who Davey Hattingsford is, and I think you were there to do more than that."

Atticus pulled his rolling suitcase upright next to him as his relaxed face morphed into a cold, hard stare. "You know nothing. And I'd be careful of what you say next, if you know what's good for you."

Sarah continued, "Davey told us what you said."

A set of stiletto heels clicked-clacked toward her and Atticus.

"I'm ready, Uncle Attie."

Sarah twirled around to see the beautiful bombshell who had been Rufus's assistant, the woman she had met at Patricia's Tea Room.

Confusion washed over Sarah. "Bebe?"

The woman's hypnotizing green eyes bore into Sarah's. Then she smiled, shoving her cell phone into her back pocket. She cocked her head and gave her best smile. "I heard you finally captured Rufus's killer."

Sarah waved her words away. "Wait," Sarah said, her eyes darting from the young lady to the old man. She pointed at both of them. "He's your uncle?"

Bebe's smile faded. "Yeah." She paused a moment before adding, "So?"

"So, you were in this together," Sarah said.

Bebe snickered. "What? What are you talking about?"

Without tearing his gaze from Sarah, Atticus said, "Bebe, don't say another word."

"Why?" Bebe crossed her arms, her head bobbing

back and forth slightly with self-satisfaction. Her lips formed a hard smile as she locked eyes with Sarah. "We didn't do anything wrong. Rufus was a disgruntled old man who was way past his prime and thought he could perform his final act without me."

"Wait. He fired you?" It was starting to come together for Sarah.

Bebe exchanged glances with her uncle but remained quiet.

"So, you were both fired by Rufus," Sarah said. She regarded Atticus again. "And you told Buster about his brother sabotaging his show, and Davey about how Rufus knew he was head-over-heels in love with Judy before he stole her from him."

"I think they had a right to know," Atticus said, trying to sidestep around Sarah.

Sarah moved in front of him, blocking his path. "Of course, but why now?"

Atticus looked down his nose at her. "Surely, I had kept those secrets long enough."

"You kept those secrets until your niece, Bebe, was fired."

"You don't understand," Bebe said. "He promised me a big bonus with glowing recommendations after his retirement. I was dedicated to him all these years."

"She did everything for him," Atticus continued.

"And he treated her terribly. Long hours, no breaks, and then he has the gall to fire her after she faints from exhaustion. Says she couldn't cut it."

Bebe shook her head in disappointment. "Stripped me of my best years and took away my future. He was a vile man who knew what he was doing. Promising me everything until the very last performance, so that I would be committed, then he pulled the rug out from under me."

"As horrible as that is," Sarah said, "what you did was worse. You should be arrested."

Atticus snickered. "For what? We didn't commit a crime."

"But you knew that this information could cause one of the brothers to commit the act. You knew one of them would do the bidding for you."

Atticus grumbled with annoyance. "I knew nothing. I only let the cat out of the bag. The rest isn't on us. I didn't tell Davey to kill. So, there's nothing you can pin on us."

Sarah narrowed her eyes. "You're right. You didn't tell Davey to kill. But you knew we were closing in on him, and you were afraid that Davey would start talking. Perhaps even tie you right into this mess."

Atticus laughed. "Talk about what? Like I said, we did nothing."

Sarah leaned back into her heels before placing her hands on her hips. "This was your plan all along. You knew you couldn't get the money from Rufus. But with him dead, the fortune would go to his wife, and with Davey's connection to Judy, you knew she would help him any way she could. You were blackmailing Davey."

"We were only there to collect the money that was owed to us."

"Now you're skipping town before Davey starts talking."

Bebe scoffed, sliding her black sunglasses over her eyes and fluffing her hair. "Let's go, Uncle Attie. We don't need this."

Atticus grabbed his bag, swinging it over his shoulder, and he grasped the handle of his suitcase.

A familiar voice from behind her spoke, startling her. "So, you *did* lie to the police."

Ignoring the shock written all over Atticus and Bebe's faces, Sarah swiveled her head toward the voice. "Adam? What are you doing here?"

"I followed you. Emma was worried that you might be heading for trouble. Said you told her that you were going to check something out. I put it all together. I knew you were going to the Dolphin Motel to find Atticus."

"I'm so glad you're here. Arrest them." Sarah pointed at Atticus and Bebe.

Atticus let out a timid chuckle. "You can't do that."

"Sure, we can," Sheriff Wheeler said, appearing from around the corner, where Adam had been. Next to him was Officer Finley. "And we heard the whole thing. Blackmail, lying to law enforcement, impeding the investigation."

Adam nodded. "Those are some serious offenses."

Bebe glanced over at her uncle, who crossed his arms. "You can't prove anything," he said.

"Oh," Adam said with a wide grin. "I think phone records and a gander at your bank accounts would clear this all right up."

Atticus's eyes went wide, and before anyone could blink, the huge man took off, leaving his bags behind as he plowed between the sheriff and the police officer standing in his way. Both law officers were knocked off their feet, falling like bowling pins in opposite directions.

"Uncle Attie!" Bebe shrieked, watching as Adam was hot on her uncle's heels. She dropped her own bags, ready to run after him.

"Oh, no, you don't!" Sarah pressed the toe of her sneaker into the back of the woman's heel, causing her to fall. Sheriff Wheeler scrambled to apprehend the woman on the ground.

"Help Dunkin!" Wheeler shouted to his officer.

Officer Finley was already on his feet, but only made a few strides in their direction when the doorman locked the door just in time for Atticus's face to slam into the glass, leaving a squashed-up facial imprint, before tumbling onto his back.

Adam hopped on top of the man, quickly rolling him over to his stomach to grab his hands. "I guess we can add assaulting an officer and resisting arrest to your rap sheet."

Atticus grumbled as Adam grasped both of his wrists, tying them behind him.

As Officer Finley took over for Sheriff Wheeler and apprehended Bebe, she struggled against him. "Uh, get off of me!"

Sarah watched as Finley grappled for her wrists. She couldn't help but smile in pure amusement as the two were being handcuffed.

Sheriff Wheeler strutted up next to Sarah and patted her shoulder. "I don't know how you do it, young lady, but I'm starting to think you have a gift."

Sarah turned to the Sheriff. "I don't know if it's a gift so much as it is an obsession for justice."

"That's what makes a good detective. Maybe you should consider the force?"

Sarah shook her head. The last thing she ever wanted was to be stuck in an office, or worse, attend any sort of bootcamp. She hated running. "No, thank you. I'll stick to selling cute puppy attire and toys at my grandpa's pet boutique."

In front of Sarah, Bebe struggled against Officer Finley as he pulled her up to her feet.

"Let me go!" she demanded.

"Looks like you'll be enjoying not only your first Christmas in Florida, but also in jail," Sarah said as Bebe was led out of the hotel barefoot by Officer Finley.

CHAPTER 24

"Pick a card, any card!" Larry fanned out a standard fifty-two-card deck in front of his granddaughters.

It was now Christmas Eve, a few days after Sarah and Adam had apprehended the people involved in Rufus's murder, and now the town was quiet and twinkling with lights and holiday cheer. Larry insisted on keeping the shop's door open for anyone who wanted to stop in for merry wishes and an ornament gift, and Sarah was glad that they had.

So far, Henry Fudderman had stopped by for Herbie, the turtle, and dropped off his infamous Boardwalk Fudge Cakes and two bags of Fudderman's dog treats wrapped in green and red foil for the pups. Patricia and Nancy had also come, bearing a box full of flaky, buttery pastries and a tin filled with holiday spiced tea.

In exchange, the Shores family offered them triple-chocolate peppermint cupcakes, a treat that Sarah had baked from her grandmother's recipe book, as well as shiny pet ornaments to hang in their homes. But after that, other than the Christmas music that filled the store, it had been a very quiet day.

Winston was lying on his side behind the counter in his corner, his legs kicking now and then as he dreamt. Rugby was sprawled out on the other side of the counter behind Larry, his chin resting on the floor, brows up, shifting his gaze from one person to the next as they spoke.

Emma groaned. "Not another magic trick, Grandpa," she said to her grandfather, who was waiting anxiously with the full deck of cards spread out in front of him.

Misty leapt from Emma's lap onto her cozy spot on the top shelf in the boutique and let out a long yawn before curling up and nuzzling herself into a ball of fluff.

"My sentiments exactly," Emma said.

Sarah nudged her cousin.

"C'mon," Larry said, bouncing slightly on his toes. "Pick a card!"

Emma rolled her eyes. "Okay, okay." She picked a

card, clutching it by its corner and sliding it out carefully.

Larry grinned with excitement. "Take a good look at it. Memorize your card."

Emma showed it to Sarah—an eight of hearts.

"Now put it back into the deck," Larry said, motioning with the cards.

Emma followed her grandfather's orders and stuck the card back with the others.

"Perfect!" Larry said, tidying up the deck into a nice stack. "Now, I'm going to shuffle them." He split the cards in half and awkwardly positioned them, bending them with his thumb. As he released them, they ruffled and dozens of cards flew into the air, landing on the floor at his feet.

"I know this trick!" Emma said. "It's called fifty-two pickup." She doubled over in laughter.

"Darn it!" Larry disappeared behind the counter as he knelt to pick up the cards. "It's not over yet," he said, index finger peeking up from behind the counter.

The bells jingled over the door and a medium-built man with a tweed suit and a flat cap strolled in.

"Orlando Prince," Sarah said. "What are you doing here?"

Orlando took off his hat as he walked in. "Merry Christmas."

Larry rose, straightening himself, all his cards collected from the floor now in his hand. "Orlando Prince! What a nice surprise!"

Orlando smiled in greeting. "Thank you." He glanced at Sarah. "I wanted to stop by and thank you for everything."

"Can I get you anything, Mr. Prince?" Larry asked. "Some tea?"

"I am feeling a bit parched." Orlando tugged the collar of his shirt. "A glass of water, if it's not too much trouble."

"Of course. I'll get that for you right away!" Larry put down the cards and rushed out of the room to retrieve his guest's beverage.

Sarah sashayed around the counter. "There's no need to thank me."

"Oh, but I must," Orlando said. "You were the only one who believed that I didn't do it. If it weren't for you, I'd still be stuck in that cell, and worse, over the holiday. You know, I didn't have anyone to bail me out."

Sarah smiled with appreciation. Then she motioned to the red handkerchief in his front pocket. "I see you got your handkerchief back."

Orlando looked at his breast pocket. "Oh, no, the police still have it. I just replaced it." He patted his chest.

Sarah furrowed her eyebrows. Why in the world

would he replace a handkerchief that didn't match his suit?

Larry arrived with a glass of water and handed it to Orlando.

Orlando rubbed his hands together before taking the glass. "Thank you, sir." He held up the glass and eyed it a moment. "What a perfect, crystal-clear glass of water. I bet it's as good as it looks." Making a show of it, he took a sip, wiping his lips with the back of his hand. "Ah, yes. Very delicious."

Sarah and Emma exchanged perturbed glances with each other.

Orlando regarded them all. "Just a typical glass of water, right?"

They all nodded in agreement.

Then Orlando set the glass on the counter and pulled the red silk handkerchief from his pocket.

Emma leaned into Sarah and whispered, "What's this guy's deal?"

"I don't know," Sarah said with a shrug. "Maybe he really likes water."

Orlando unfolded his handkerchief and held it up, turning it from one side to the other. "Just a regular ol' handkerchief, right?"

"Oh, boy," Emma said. "Is this a magic trick?" She leaned in closer.

"It sure is." Orlando covered the glass with the handkerchief. "Larry, would you like to do the honors?"

Larry's eyes went wide with excitement. "Me? Would I?" He rushed over to the glass that was now covered. "What do you want me to do?"

Orlando stepped back. "Pull the handkerchief off the glass."

Larry inched forward and pinched the corner of the handkerchief, swiping it off the glass to reveal the same glass of water, only this time there was something in it. Something yellow, swimming angelically in circles.

"Oh my!" Emma said. "Is that a goldfish?"

Larry inspected the handkerchief in his hands. "How did you do that?"

Orlando grinned, rocking back on his heels. "A magician never tells." Then he turned to Larry. "Don't you have a trick?"

Emma, still staring at the goldfish, swept her hand toward them. "He's still practicing."

Larry lowered himself to Emma's eye level. "Oh, but I didn't finish my trick."

Emma's eyes met Larry's. "What do you mean?"

Larry motioned for Sarah and Emma to join him on the other side of the counter. When they gathered next to their grandfather, he put two fingers in his mouth and let out a sharp whistle.

Rugby came out from his corner and galloped over.

"Hey," Sarah said, pointing at the yellow lab. "He's got something in his mouth."

Larry snapped his fingers. "Drop it."

Rugby dropped the card at Emma's feet, and it lay faceup.

Emma froze, her eyes blinking rapidly in disbelief. "Eight of hearts."

Larry crossed his arms in front of himself, a smirk creeping onto his face. Pointing at it on the floor, he asked, "Was that your card?"

Emma's mouth hung open. After several seconds of pure shock, she bent over and picked it up. "But...how?"

"I got a little help from Orlando Prince here. He taught me a few tricks yesterday when you two were doing your final Christmas shopping."

"A few tricks?" Emma said. "Grandpa, that was amazing!"

"It sure is!" Sarah said. "Grandpa, but how did you do it?"

Larry glanced at Orlando, who was grinning wide. Then he turned back to his granddaughters. "A magician never tells," he said with a wink.

Sarah chuckled. "Of course."

"Orlando Prince and Buster Hattingsford are partnering up to do a two-man magic show," Larry said.

"And they asked if I would be a part of it whenever they tour here in Cascade Cove." He puffed out his chest with pride and grinned.

Sarah regarded Orlando. "That's amazing news! I wish you all luck!"

Orlando waved his hands in front of himself. "We won't need it. Buster and I are dedicated. I have no doubt we can make a name for ourselves. Like I said to Larry here, all you need is practice."

"And a beautiful assistant," Emma added.

They all laughed.

Orlando wagged his finger at her, still holding his jiggling belly with the other. "Maybe one of them, too."

CHAPTER 25

Snug under her warm blanket in a deep holiday slumber, something jostled Sarah. By the level of darkness behind her eyelids, it couldn't have been morning yet. Maybe she'd dreamt it. She decided to drift off again.

"Wake up!"

The voice sounded familiar, but Sarah was too tired to identify who it was.

She heard the voice a second time.

"Sarah!"

Sarah groaned and rolled over to face the person who was disturbing her deep dreams. She forced her eyes open. Whoever was interrupting her sleep was still fuzzy, though she could make out the blonde bun on top of the head of this particular person, and that gave the person's identity away.

"Emma, what are you doing? The sun isn't even up yet."

"Sarah, it's Christmas morning. Presents!"

"What are you, like, ten?"

Emma nudged her some more. "Sarah, c'mon. Santa Claus was here."

"Grow up," Sarah said, before pulling the covers over her head.

Sarah was just nuzzling herself comfortably back to sleep when a bright light jolted her. But before she could contemplate exactly how she would murder her own cousin for turning on the light, someone or something jumped onto her bed.

"Up and at 'em!"

It was a different voice. Sarah removed the covers from her head and turned to see not only her grandfather, but Winston's tongue and Rugby's huge nose in her face.

Larry was still in his lobster pajamas, his hair disheveled from a good night's sleep. "It's Christmas morning! Santy Claus was here!"

"Oh." Sarah nudged the dogs out of her face and regarded her grandfather. "Not you too!"

Emma laughed. "I told you. Grandpa does not take

Christmas mornings lightly. Now everyone is up. Let's go!"

Sarah had no choice but to throw the covers off of herself and slip into her robe and slippers. She followed her grandfather and cousin into the living room, where they had set up a bushy sand pine tree. Her grandfather had gone out of his way to make sure Sarah had the best first Christmas in Florida, and he had driven over an hour to a small tree farm in Deltona to get a real tree for Sarah, even though she insisted it was okay to set up the aluminum tree in the box that was tucked away in the attic. It was a little more expensive than Sarah had expected, but Larry had explained that in order for them to have a real tree for Christmas, they had to pay a little extra because the trees had to be trucked in from up north.

She inhaled the aroma of tangerines and pine that the tree gave off in the room, and it definitely reminded her of Christmas up north. After inhaling the tantalizing aroma, she noticed all the presents displayed under the tree. There were definitely more boxes under that tree than the night before. "Wow, you weren't kidding."

"Told you Santa was here," Larry said, his nose up in the air as he made his way into the kitchen. "Coffee will be ready in five minutes."

The morning was bursting with celebration as they

exchanged gifts, tearing away fragments of Christmas paper of all sizes and leaving it on the floor without a care.

Sarah ripped open a box and held up a pair of blue footed pajamas with penguins and snowflakes. She raised an eyebrow. "Really?"

"That's from me," Emma said with a chuckle.

"But the tag says it's from Santa."

"Oh, right. From Santa," Emma corrected herself. "There's more in there."

Sarah laid down the pajamas and shuffled through the tissue paper to find another pair of pajamas that matched the first, only this one was smaller. Sarah cocked her head.

"That's for Winston. Matching PJs since he likes to sneak into bed with you." Emma giggled again. "I couldn't find Rugby's size."

Sarah laughed. "Thank you." She stood and bent over to pick up two gifts, one for each dog, and placed them in front of them. She tapped the boxes. "Go on. Open your gifts," she said, tearing a corner for each of them to get started.

Rugby and Winston sniffed their respective presents before pawing at them and eventually tearing the paper with their teeth. Misty, on the other hand, wasn't keen on opening gifts. Instead, she sat as if she were on a throne, licking her paw and watching the two heathens act like animals.

Misty was given a stuffed mouse that wore small bells that jingled and what seemed like a year's worth of catnip, most likely a bulk order from one of the shop's suppliers.

Rugby and Winston were given many toys and treats, but their big gift was an interactive ball thrower, which Sarah felt slightly concerned about. Knowing that Rugby could act a little crazy at times, she wasn't sure how he would react to such a contraption.

After opening presents, they ate breakfast and watched the dogs play with their new toys. Misty was sitting in the middle of the floor, batting Rugby over the head every time he galloped past her.

Larry got up to his feet and surveyed the mess in the living room. "Guess it's time to clean up." He grabbed a trash bag to haul all the garbage into and the two girls got busy collecting the scraps of wrapping paper off the floor. As they were finishing cleaning up, there was a knock at the door.

Larry put down the trash bag. "Wonder who that could be." He sauntered over and looked through the peephole. "Look what the cat dragged in," he said, opening the door.

Mark and Adam walked in.

Emma jumped up, adjusting the messy bun on her head. "Mark? What are you doing here? I thought you were spending Christmas with your family."

He walked over to her briskly and gave her a hug. After they parted from their embrace, Mark said, "Well, Aunt Althea lit her hair on fire by accident."

Emma and Sarah gasped simultaneously.

"What?" Emma asked, lowering her hands down from her mouth. "How?"

Mark inhaled sharply. "She tried to light a Virginia Slim and, well, with the amount of Aqua Net she uses on her bouffant hairstyle..." Mark shrugged matter-of-factly. "It was bound to happen."

"Is she okay?" Sarah asked.

Mark nodded. "More than okay. She's extra feisty."

"Smoking?" Emma asked. "I thought she quit."

"Apparently not. My mom tried to stop her, but it was too late. After the nest on top of her head went up in smoke, everyone thought it would be best if we all just went home—including Aunt Althea. They checked her into the hospital," Mark said. Then he rolled his eyes. "Kicking and screaming, of course. Anyway, I got you something." He handed Emma a small gift. "It was a little last minute."

Emma nodded as she opened the box. "Oh." She

pulled out what looked like an herb with several red berries and held it up.

Mark inched closer to her. "It's mistletoe."

Emma's cheeks flushed, and she let out a nervous giggle. "I know that! But why would you—"

Mark took the mistletoe from her, holding it up with one hand and drawing Emma in close to him with the other. Emma put her arms around his neck, and they kissed.

Larry folded his hands together in front of him. "Have you ever seen something so romantic?"

Sarah smiled warmly. She couldn't be more happy for her cousin. Mark really was perfect for her.

Adam approached her, clearing his throat. "I got something for you, too."

"Oh, hold that thought." Sarah ran into the other room and grabbed a present that she had hidden under her bed. She brought it out into the living room where Adam stood. She handed him his gift, complete with a big red bow on top. "This is for you," she said.

Adam took the present and unwrapped it, slower than Sarah had expected. When he opened the box, he glanced up at her, lifting an eyebrow quizzically. "What's this?" He pulled out a stress ball.

Sarah smiled. "It's for when you're on the job. And for when I come in like a hurricane and mix things up."

Adam chuckled, squeezing the ball in his hand. "You could never mess things up." He put the ball back into its box and pulled out a present for Sarah. "Here, this is for you." He handed her the small gift, wrapped in a gold ribbon.

Sarah grinned. She untied the bow, sliding the sash off the gift, and opened the box. Her eyes went wide when she saw what was inside.

Adam beamed. "Now you'll never have bad luck on Christmas."

It was a gold flamingo pendant with a ruby Santa hat and a few tiny diamonds as the trim of the hat. There was also one big diamond, acting as the white ball at the end.

Eyes wide, Sarah murmured, "A flamingo with a Santa hat." She bobbed the piece back and forth slightly and it caught the light, glistening. Then she furrowed her eyebrows. "Is this real?"

Adam turned white. "Uh, well, sort of. It's fourteen-karat."

"The diamonds look real."

"Oh, yeah, they're real, too. But it was the best flamingo with a Santa hat I could find and it's...well, you can wear it."

"Adam," Sarah said in shock. "This is too much."

Adam knitted his brow in worry. "Sarah, you are my

best friend and you helped me. If it weren't for you, I wouldn't be a detective. And I wouldn't have been able to solve the mystery of who murdered Rufus without you. This is a token of my gratitude and friendship. I wanted to show you how much you mean to me." Adam's face relaxed as he smiled. "Besides, this necklace will always remind you of your first Florida Christmas."

Sarah tilted her head slightly. "It's beautiful, Adam."

Adam sighed in relief. "I'm glad you like it."

"I love it," Sarah said, her eyes now glued to his. She wrapped her arms around him and squeezed. Without thought, she kissed him on the cheek. "Thank you."

When they pulled back from their embrace, Adam stared into her eyes for a moment, until Larry interrupted. "I'm making a big Christmas dinner, with ham, filling, and sweet potatoes. Would you fine men like to join us?"

Mark rubbed his tummy. "Would I?"

Emma laughed.

Adam stepped toward Larry. "I'm in, too."

"Great! Anyone want to help me with the pie?" Larry eyed Sarah.

Sarah shook her head and let out a chuckle. "I guess it's up to me to bake the pie."

Larry bounced up and down. "You're the best! You know how my baking is."

"Yes, Grandpa," Emma said. "We all know!"

Everyone followed Larry into the kitchen to help make the best Christmas dinner for the five of them.

Sarah hung back a moment, staring at the lights that glistened on the tree. Winston leaned into her leg. "I know, Winston. It's your first Christmas in Cascade Cove, too. How do you like it so far?"

She bent down to pat him on the head, and he gave her a wet kiss.

"Me too, Winston," she said as she listened to everyone chattering in the kitchen. Then she heard a tray clatter onto the floor, followed by Grandpa Larry yelling, "No, Rugby! Drop it!"

Sarah chuckled as she rubbed Winston's ears. "And I hope we have many more just like it."

# # #

Thank you for reading! Want to help out?

Reviews are a big help for independent authors like me, so if you liked my book, **please consider leaving a review today**.

Thank you!

-Mel McCoy

ABOUT THE AUTHOR

Mel McCoy has had a lifelong love of mysteries of all kinds. Reading everything from Nancy Drew to the Miss Marple series and obsessed with shows like *Murder, She Wrote,* her love of the genre has never wavered.

Now she is hoping to spread her love of mysteries through her new Whodunit Pet Cozy Mystery Series. Centered around a cozy beachside town, the series features a cast of interesting characters and their pets, along with antiques, crafts such as knitting, and plenty of culinary delights.

Mel lives with her two dogs, a rambunctious and bossy Yorkie named Peanut, and a dopey, lazy hound (who snores a lot!) named Murph.

For more info on Mel McCoy's cozy mystery series, please visit: www.melmccoybooks.com

Connect with Mel:

Facebook: facebook.com/CozyMysteryMel
Twitter: twitter.com/CozyMysteryMel

WANT A FREE STORY?

Grab your free copy of *The Case of the Ominous Corgi*, a short cozy mystery featuring Rugby, Winston, and Misty. Simply visit www.melmccoybooks.com and click the "Free Story" link.

Made in the USA
Monee, IL
16 December 2019